NATALIE LLOYD

the KEY to EXTRAORDINARY

Scholastic Inc.

Copyright © 2016 by Natalie Lloyd

This book was originally published in hardcover by Scholastic Press in 2016.

All rights reserved. Published by Scholastic Inc., *Publishers since 1920*. SCHOLASTIC and associated logos are trademarks and/or registered trademarks of Scholastic Inc.

The publisher does not have any control over and does not assume any responsibility for author or third-party websites or their content.

No part of this publication may be reproduced, stored in a retrieval system, or transmitted in any form or by any means, electronic, mechanical, photocopying, recording, or otherwise, without written permission of the publisher. For information regarding permission, write to Scholastic Inc., Attention: Permissions Department, 557 Broadway, New York, NY 10012.

ISBN 978-0-545-55276-9

10 9 8 7 6 5 4 3 2 1   17 18 19 20 21

Printed in the U.S.A.   40
First printing 2017

Book design by Nina Goffi

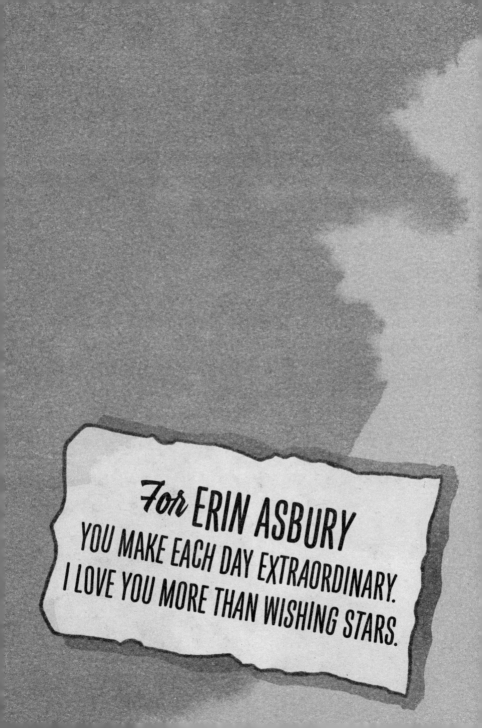

For ERIN ASBURY
YOU MAKE EACH DAY EXTRAORDINARY.
I LOVE YOU MORE THAN WISHING STARS.

CHAPTER ONE

It is a known fact that the most extraordinary moments in a person's life come disguised as ordinary days.

It is a known fact for me, at least.

Because that morning started out mostly the same as all mornings before: I woke up to an ache in my chest, the smell of chocolate, and the sound of the ghost making a racket in the kitchen.

Now, I'm not the sort to dwell on doom and sorrow. Life is too short for that. But I should at least try to describe the ache briefly:

It's not the kind that comes from eating tacos too late at night.

It's the kind that comes from being left behind.

I think my heart knows I should be filling it with new memories, new jokes, and wondrous adventures with the one person I loved most of all. But that person is gone now.

And so, my heart has a giant hole in it. I call it the Big Empty.

I squeezed my eyes shut and reminded myself of these affirmations:

Tonight you could have your Destiny Dream.

Never doubt your starry aim.

I repeated those words while I tugged my mud boots on over my jeans, and again when I zipped up my favorite hoodie. Early summer had settled into the mountains, but the air was still chilly first thing in the morning. I didn't feel cold, though. I felt energized. Just the prospect of my Destiny Dream rattled my brain to such a degree that I fixed my sideways braid on the wrong side of my head. I'm not superstitious about most things, but I knew the day would go badly if I wore my braid on the wrong side.

Finally, I snatched up my messenger bag and zoomed down the stairs to see what the ghost was up to.

Since there's no sense in scaring a ghost who might whirl around and scare me in turn, I decided to declare myself.

"It's Emma!" I called out as I stepped into the darkness of the Boneyard Cafe.

My family's bakery, the Boneyard Cafe, takes up the whole bottom floor of our house, which is perched on the edge of a famous cemetery, hence the cafe's creeptastical name. Currently, Granny Blue is doing her best to keep the Boneyard running, as business hasn't been too great lately.

"I'm back here," yelled a voice that, unfortunately, belonged to my big brother, Topher, and not one of the dearly departed. I'd never actually seen the ghost in our kitchen; I'd only heard it banging around. But due to my home's location, I figure I'm bound to run into a ghost eventually.

The air was thick with the smell of chocolate as I walked into the kitchen. The Cocoa Cauldron was already bubbling near the far window. It was Topher's week to make Boneyard Brew, our cafe's most famous treat. As near as I can describe it, Boneyard Brew is like hot chocolate with a heavenly twist. Maybe it seems crazy to drink hot chocolate in the summer, but I'm here to tell you: Once you've had a taste of Boneyard Brew, you'll never stop craving it. Topher even makes homemade marshmallows.

The marshmallow man himself was perched on the tip-top of the tall ladder, digging through one of the supply cabinets like a scrawny snack bandit.

"Hungry?" I asked him.

Thomp. Topher bumped his head on the cabinet, and let out a low groan. He got all squinty-eyed, pretending to be mad, as he hunkered down to look at me. But I could see the start of a smile on his face. "Emma Pearl Casey, I thought you might be a ghost."

"I yelled and declared myself!"

"I know." Topher gave me the same dimpled-cheek grin that made most of the girls at Blackbird Hollow Community

College go googly-eyed. "I always get skittish when I'm down here before daylight."

"It *is* early for you to be making brew," I agreed. In my nearly twelve years of existence, we'd never opened before ten a.m. on Sundays.

"I can't get this recipe out of my head," Topher said by way of explanation. "Peach-lavender muffins. I won't have any peace of mind until I make them. And I thought I'd get the brew going while I was down here."

"I'm glad you're making extra. I usually have a big tour group in the graveyard on Sunday."

Topher cocked his head and studied my face. "Are you okay? You look . . . troubled."

I gave him a thumbs-up. "All good."

"Huh." He didn't look convinced, but he reached back into the cabinet and dislodged one of the giant silver muffin pans. He twisted out of the way as it clattered to the floor.

"Easy!" I said as I jumped to hand it back to him. "If you make any more noise down here, you'll—"

"What? Wake the dead? You and Blue play music so loud the dead can't get any sleep around here anyway."

"I was going to say wake my *dog*. But that's a fair point about the loud music."

Topher stretched tall again, and got back to digging. He tossed a sack of Blue's organic flour down on the counter-top before he dismounted the rickety ladder. I could tell by the tune he was whistling that Topher was about to go into a serious baking frenzy. He'd already tied his red bandana securely around his head. That was a direct order from Granny Blue. Topher likes to let his hair grow long and shaggy for summer, so Blue makes him pull his hair back when he bakes.

I felt a soft thump-thump-thump against my boot, and looked down to see Bearclaw yawning up at me. I scooped her up into my arms and hugged her against my chest.

When Topher took me to the animal shelter to pick out a pup, the lady said we didn't want *That Dog* because she was scrawny. But I knew from the first time I saw That Dog, she was meant to be mine. I hope every person in the world gets to have an experience so wondrous: the sweet tug at your heart when you look at a dog, and a dog looks at you, and you know you're meant to take care of each other.

Topher thought I made a fine choice in picking That Dog but we both decided she needed a bolder name, something that'd help her see herself in a new way. So I named her the toughest word I could think of: *Bearclaw.*

I call her Bear for short.

That day at the shelter, Bear leaped up into my arms as soon as I called out her name, as if she'd been waiting her whole life for someone to see her true potential.

"Good morning, my fearless little fuzz monster," I whispered against her floppy ear.

Bear nuzzled happily against my neck.

"Is Granny Blue still sleeping?" I asked.

"I don't think she sleeps much anymore." Topher stirred the big spoon through the Boneyard Brew. He nodded toward her office. The door was closed, but a glow of yellow light seeped out into the hallway. "Her light was still on when I went to bed. I wouldn't be surprised if she stayed awake all night." Most of Blackbird Hollow was having a tough time making ends meet, and the cafe was no different.

I cuddled Bear close, but stayed in the doorway. Granny's rule is that Bear can't go in the kitchen. She says some people are particular about dog fur in their biscuits.

Topher opened a tiny jar full of dried lavender. He tap-tap-tapped out a teaspoon's worth into a tiny, sugar-filled pestle. Flour dust already graced his cheekbones, neck, and hands, as if some angel had reached down out of the clouds to trace my brother's features like, "See, now? *This* is what a perfect human looks like." We are not anything alike in that aspect, my brother and me. It would make way more sense if Topher was supposed to have the Destiny Dream.

But he wasn't.

The Destiny Dream would be happening to me. And soon, I hoped.

"Emma?" Topher studied me carefully. "I can see something's wrong. You might as well tell me."

My brother can read people like a story. He knows when a smile's covering sadness and which sparkly-eyed look is a sure sign of a secret. He can hear a broken heart in the sound of someone's voice. He's especially good at reading me. The floors creaked under Topher's sneakers as he came to stand in front of me, like he was putting himself between me and the world, as if whatever was breaking my heart would have to get past him to get to me.

"It's the Big Empty," I whispered, cuddling Bear tight against the infernal ache in my chest. "I woke up thinking that I wanted to talk to Mama. And then I realized I couldn't talk to her and . . ." I shrugged. "It aches, is all. Missing her is a terrible ache."

Topher reached out to hug me, but I spun around and headed for the back door.

"I'm fine, Toph. No need to start the day all morbid and sad. Anyway, I'm off to see the long-ago dearly departed."

I made my way through the kitchen door and onto the back porch. The screen door slapped shut behind me, and I stared out over the dreamy-morning world. The dark night had already faded to a pretty, pale blue at the horizon. A cool wind prickled my skin and rustled the branches of the big oak in the center of the field. It was a life sound the wind made, a pretty rasp and then *shhh* . . . which was kind of strange considering all that lay before me. As far as I could see, the headstones and statues of Blackbird Hollow Cemetery peeked up from the mist.

I plucked a white daisy from the grass, stuck it in my braid, and set out to walk among those graves, just the same as always. I only walk in the daylight, though. Everybody in town knows you never set foot in Blackbird Hollow Cemetery at night. Most people are too skitter-brained to go there during the day as well. But I'm not afraid.

Not exactly.

Okay, here's the honest truth: Sometimes I do feel like something is following me around in the graveyard. At times, that feeling comforts me; it's like I'm being watched over. But every now and then, I get a certain chill and feel more like I'm being flat-out watched.

I was right about both things. But I didn't know it yet.

CHAPTER TWO

Bear jumped out of my arms so she could scamper ahead of me through the graveyard. I stopped at the first crooked stone rising up out of the mist, reached deep into my bag, and pulled out a cluster of dried-up flowers from the day before. I tucked them against the base of the stone.

"Someone loved you, Adeline Carpetta," I whispered.

Most people think my backyard is haunted. I suppose that's understandable, considering my backyard also happens to be one of the oldest cemeteries in the state of Tennessee. But it's also quiet and sacred and full of shady trees, stone angels, and names. Old, beautiful names that sound like they dripped out of a storybook:

Adeline Carpetta

Captain Daniel Toliver, 1st Tennessee Infantry

Wonder St. Clare

Cillian McNeal

Mama said if I ever felt lonesome in a graveyard, I should say the names on the stones aloud and declare the better truth of the situation, like this:

"Someone loved you, Wonder St. Clare."

Granny Blue doesn't believe in ghosts the way most people in town do. She says it's memories that haunt people. "I can't imagine the afterlife is so boring people have to keep pestering you from the Great Beyond," she said. But whenever I walk through Blackbird Hollow Cemetery and I call out the names on the stones, I always feel . . . something. I know they aren't here, those folks. But I believe they're somewhere. And maybe what I feel is their happiness when they pull back the curtain and take a look at what's happening back here on earth.

Bear nudged her head underneath my palm. I leaned down, cupped her fuzzy face, and kissed her soft ear. That's when I heard the flutter of friendly chatter. The old gates are the public entry point, and I was excited to see a good-size group waiting for me.

A happy shiver settled over my shoulders as I stood and looked toward the noise. The fog was fading now, lifting up out of the cemetery in curls and wisps. Clusters of bright dandelions bloomed open—one at a time—in a perfectly curved path all the way to the gate.

"Good morning!" I called out as I scampered down the hill. Bear yapped as she bounded along beside me.

"Good morning, Emma Pearl!" yelled some of the folks standing at the gate.

Once upon a time, the gates were probably beautiful. Nobody knows for sure, because now they're covered by a thick fluff of coppery rust. Waxy vines of ivy wrap through the bars and up around the spires. Ivy grows everywhere in the cemetery. It dangles from the giant oak trees and creeps across the mossy tombstones. It's tangled so thick around the fence that passersby can barely see inside. Sometimes I think the mountains and the woods might be in cahoots, using their ivy powers to hide Blackbird Hollow from the world. To keep it sacred, maybe.

Or to keep it all secret.

I cranked my gate key sideways in the lock, until I heard the satisfying click. The gates swung open slowly, emitting a long, low *screeeeech*.

At least twenty people were waiting for me, mostly white-haired retired folks, all milling around talking to one another. The couple at the front of the line were my regulars: an old man with a long white beard, and an elderly lady on a sassy pink scooter.

They're also my relatives: Granny Blue's brother, Periwinkle, and his wife, Greta.

"Welcome to Blackbird Hollow Cemetery!" I called out as I pushed the gate open. "One of the oldest and most famous resting-places in the state!"

The air filled with a clatter of applause. They always applaud, though I'm not sure why. Everybody there'd heard my speech plenty of times. But I like giving folks the full-tour experience. "This morning's excursion is our famous Love Tour. Your journey through our town's great and glorious romantic past will last approximately seven minutes."

I fished down into my tote bag and began passing out pairs of heart-shaped sunglasses to my guests.

"Now, these are fancy, Emma!" said Uncle Periwinkle as he slid on the shades. He lifted his paper cup of Boneyard Brew in salute.

"You're lucky Topher was up early on Brew Duty," I told him. "It's never ready before the sun rises."

"He must have known I'd need a fix." Uncle Periwinkle grinned. His long white beard billowed in the breeze. Were it not for his faded jeans and raggedy jacket—or the big, sweet smile on his face—Uncle Periwinkle would look a bit ghostly himself. Most days, he pins a tiny flower over his heart. But today, he'd decided to get festive. He'd tucked a violet into his beard.

Uncle Peri leaned down and said softly, "I don't need heart-shaped spectacles to see something's bothering you." He patted my shoulder. "What's that sad look in your eyes all about?"

"Restless night."

"What?!" Aunt Greta screeched. She grabbed my arm and, to her credit, tried to whisper but mostly yelled, "Restless night? Emma, did you have your Destiny Dream?!"

"Ha!" Uncle Peri clapped his hands. "I knew her mama was right! What have I always told you, Greta? I said, 'See now, Emma's going to have her Destiny Dream early!' "

I reached out and gave them both a gentle shake. "You guys, *shhh*! I haven't had the dream. Not yet. The Big Empty kept me up all night. That's all I meant."

"Ah." Periwinkle nodded. A grin tugged at his beard. "That happens around here when seasons change, you know. People remember the ones they love and miss."

Uncle Periwinkle fancies himself the town historian. For many years, he worked as the newspaper editor. According to Granny Blue, being a newspaper editor in a town this size is just a fancy way of saying he minded everybody's business but his own.

Aunt Greta grabbed my arm and yanked me close for a hard hug. She smelled like roses and hair spray. "You'll have your Destiny Dream soon enough, sugar. Now why don't you let me hold that wild dog while you give your tour?" Bear jumped up into Greta's lap, thrilled for the invite. "*Hmpfh!*" Greta groaned as Bear licked her chin.

I'd never seen Aunt Greta actually smile. She only ever pressed her mouth into a firm line and made a *hmpfh* noise when she was happy.

Ever since she broke her hip last year, Aunt Greta's been rambling all over town on a customized pink scooter. This morning was no exception. She wore a pink tracksuit to match her ride, and her white hair was tucked up into a rosy-colored baseball cap. She'd stitched her flower shop's slogan onto the cap:

GRETA'S MAGICAL GARDEN:

GET YOUR FLOWERS—THEN GO AWAY

"Thank you, everyone, for coming out this morning," I said as I made my way down the line, passing a pair of sunglasses to Mr. Marcum and his wife. The Marcums had won Farmers of the Year going on twenty-seven years now. Last year, their ten-pound tomato made the front page of the *Regional Farmers' Almanac*. In the world of competitive tomato farming, the Marcums are total rock stars.

"We're tickled to be here, Emma!" Mrs. Marcum hugged me tight before she donned her shades.

I cleared my throat. "If everybody's okay with it, we'll start early this morning. Daisies are blooming on the rooftops. That means the rain's coming."

That's another fact about Blackbird Hollow, Tennessee, that some folks attribute to the supernatural: Flowers never stop blooming here. They bloom through the snow. They bloom up through cracks in concrete sidewalks. They bloom in bundles near the river, and in colorful bursts in yards and hillsides. And they've always bloomed especially thick here in the graveyard. You'd think this place was a proper garden, were it not for all the headstones.

"HOLD UP!" shouted a young woman running across the street. "Wait for me, please!"

"Who is that?" Aunt Greta huffed, spinning her scooter around so fast the dirt spun underneath her tires. "And what's she getting so worked up about? This ain't Noah's Ark. It's just a cemetery tour."

The stranger looked about Topher's age. She was a tiny thing. But she had to be stronger than she looked, because the bulky backpack on her shoulders seemed twice her height. Even then, it didn't slow her down a step. Her hair was dark, mostly, but one bright pink stripe fell across her face. She looked cool, like a punk-rock mountain fairy.

"How much does this tour cost?" she asked as she came to stand beside me.

"There's no charge," I said brightly. "But of course we'd be grateful for a donation." I held up my tote bag so she could see the slogan embroidered on the side:

MAKE BLACKBIRD HOLLOW CEMETERY BOO-TIFUL AGAIN.

Aunt Greta made the bags for last month's fund-raiser. She didn't grin when I showed off her creation, of course. But her face flushed pink with pride.

"We do ongoing fund-raisers to maintain this graveyard," I said, passing the newcomer a pair of heart-shaped shades. Then I fished around in my tote again for the note-book. "May I have your name for our guest registry?"

"I'm Waverly Valentine."

I thought her name sounded as pretty as the names on the headstones. I didn't say that, though. Telling somebody their name would look good on a headstone might not be considered a compliment.

Uncle Periwinkle stretched out his hand to give hers a shake. "You've been hiking the Appalachian Trail, I see. Welcome to Blackbird Hollow! Stopping just for a breather or staying a while?"

Waverly glanced back toward the Wailing Woods. "Honestly, I'm not sure how I got here. The place sounds cool, though, with all the Civil War history—and stories about ghosts and treasure and . . ." She shivered. "I hadn't planned on stopping but that amazing smell pulled me in. It even *smells* magical in this town . . ."

"That's the cafe!" I pointed to my home-sweet-home. "You should go for breakfast! After the tour, of course." Few things in this life thrill me more than showing someone the graveyard for the first time. "Let's commence!"

A soft breeze settled around our shoulders as we walked into the cemetery. That same breeze made the world around us shiver a little bit. The slick green leaves of the tall trees rustled, and the long curtains of ivy dangling from the branches began to wave. When the ivy blows in the graveyard, it casts the prettiest lacelike shadows on the ground. They remind me of banners, rippling over the dearly departed in silent celebration. I pointed out the smaller stones at the front of the cemetery. And then we walked past some of my favorite memorials: the stone angel with moss-covered wings and the bronze soldier. The soldier is a monument to young men from the Hollow who died in war.

Sometimes, Aunt Greta gives me a note to tuck in the soldier's hand. I don't read what they say. One of the men who died was Aunt Greta's brother. I figure the letters are her way of remembering him.

A tremble of thunder rolled above the silver clouds, sending warning shivers up my arms.

"We might have to cut this tour short," I said as I pushed my sunglasses back into my hair.

"I have a question." Waverly twisted her hands together. "Can you tell me about the Conductor? A guy I met on the trail mentioned him to me."

The breeze died down to nothing but still air.

The restless trees hushed their whispering.

Even the thunder faded away, gently as a rock song on the radio. I felt like the whole world was listening close to what I was about to say.

"The Conductor is our most famous ghost," I said. "If you walk through the graveyard at night, or very early in the morning, some people believe you hear the Conductor's song."

Uncle Peri cleared his throat. He can't help but jump in when history's involved. "Most people think the Conductor is the ghost of a Civil War soldier who hid his loot somewhere in the hills."

Depending on the day, that thought can bring me comfort or make me tremble. By day, the graveyard is one of my favorite places to be. But sometimes I scare myself silly at night, when I lie in bed and think about the Conductor wandering among the stones, singing his lonesome song . . .

" 'The Treasure of Blackbird Hollow' is a wonderfully spooky story!" I told Waverly. "I typically save it for the Saints and Scoundrels Tour. People have tried to find the treasure for hundreds of years."

The sky rumbled again.

"Sadly, we have to end the tour when the weather gets rough," I told Waverly and the rest of my guests with a shiver. "Bearclaw is afraid of thunder."

We scampered down the hill just as the rain began plop-plop-plopping, splotching the sidewalk all around us.

"So," Waverly asked, "have you heard the Conductor sing about the treasure?"

"I don't think so," I said. "Lots of people claim they've heard him, though. I think sometimes folks want to hear him so badly they probably think they do . . . even if it's nothing more than the wind in the woods. I'd like to hear the Conductor's song, though."

It was nice to think that a song could last forever.

Uncle Peri cleared his throat. "I've heard the song."

"Peri." The way Greta said his name sounded like a warning.

"You've heard the Conductor?" I looked up into his bristly face. "You never told me that!"

"Periwinkle," Greta warned, louder this time. "Do not get carried away. You know Blue doesn't like treasure talk."

Periwinkle cleared his throat. The sky swirled silver and gray behind him. A summer storm was brewing, the kind that looked too scary for a tour . . . but just right for story-telling. "It'd be impolite not to share the story with our guest, wouldn't it? What if Miss Waverly never passes this way again? It's like this: When I was twelve years old, I came out here at night with my friends. The legend says that the Conductor won't show the treasure to somebody with bad intentions, now. He'll just lead 'em down a wrong trail, into a cave so deep they'll never get back out. I figured it was important for me to show the Conductor I was pure of heart . . ."

"Pure of heart?" Greta said. "Ha!"

Uncle Peri shrugged. "Pure-ish. So my friends and I— we walked out into the middle of the graveyard and I sang:

I'm pure of heart,
Not filled with hate,
I'll use the loot
For something great!
Oh Conductor,
At your pleasure,
Take me to your wondrous treasure!"

"Why'd you sing?" I asked.

Peri tugged on his beard. "According to legend, that's what you need to do to summon the ghost. Turns out to be true because he sang back. It went like this."

Uncle Peri clapped his hands against his pants. And he shuffled down the path toward the cafe in rhythm to his song:

"Beneath the stars of Blackbird Hollow
By the shadows of the ridge
Down a path no man can follow
Lies a treasure someone hid."

I scribbled Peri's song down on the back of the guest registry. That'd make a great detail for a future tour.

"That's the whole song?" Waverly asked.

"That's the only part I remember," Uncle Peri said. "We were so scared we ran screaming out of the graveyard and didn't even try to solve the riddle. People claim they hear all sorts of things, of course. But I heard that song with my own ears."

A purple stripe of lightning branded the skies over the faraway mountains, followed by a sharp clap of thunder.

Periwinkle held the gate open for us. "People have lost their minds trying to find that treasure," he said. "They thought if they could just find the treasure, they'd be set for life. No more hardship then. No more worries. Just the *hope* of gold makes a man do crazy things."

"Any kind of hope makes people do crazy things," Greta said. "Hope of riches. Hope of love. Hope of goodness."

"Hope of hot chocolate." Peri sniffed the air. "It's fitting Blue stirs her brew so close to this graveyard. Because I'm convinced heaven will smell like hot cocoa."

Only Waverly Valentine stayed at the gate. She stared out over the cemetery, arms wrapped tight around her chest. My heart clinched at the sad pull of her mouth.

"You should come inside, too," I told her. "Get a mug of Boneyard Brew and some breakfast. Wait out the storm. We have peach-lavender muffins this morning."

"Peach-lavender?" she breathed. She shook her head, disbelieving. "Those are my favorite muffins. I didn't know anybody else in the world made peach-lavender muffins except . . . a friend of mine. A friend I used to have."

I grinned. "No offense to your friend, but I'm certain these muffins will be the best you've ever had."

"Thanks, but I need to keep moving. You can't fight destiny." She walked away, hands clutched around her backpack straps.

I shivered all over. Even the trees seemed to shiver as the storm wind blew around us.

Destiny. That's a touchy subject in my family. I should tell you why.

It all started with a strange old book.

CHAPTER THREE

A couple of years ago, on the day I turned ten, I came to this conclusion: I think I know how it feels to fly. I don't have invisible wings blooming out of my back, or pixie dust that lifts me from one rooftop to the next. I've never even flown in an airplane.

But whenever I ride on the back of my granny Blue's motorcycle, I feel like it's only the two of us and the wild, endless air.

That's what I was doing on my tenth birthday—riding on the back of Blue's bike, with my arms locked tight around her soft middle. With the growl of the motor beneath us and the blue horizon pulling us farther ahead, I imagined we were airborne.

Flying on a rumbly storm cloud.

Flying on the back of a cool autumn wind.

It wouldn't have surprised me one bit if Blue'd popped a wheelie and driven that motorcycle straight into heaven.

Kind of like Elijah, in the Bible, with his chariot of fire. Except we'd be on a Harley-Davidson.

I rested the side of my face against Blue's back as we zoomed over the rolling hills of Blackbird Hollow. Past the old, crumbly buildings downtown. Past the curvy gravel road that led to the trailer park where my best friend, Cody Belle, lives. Blue was taking the long way home.

"Your mama's got a present for you," Blue said to me as we dismounted the bike in front of the cafe. "She's waiting for you on the back porch."

Blue pulled off her helmet, sending a waterfall of icy-white hair cascading down around her shoulders. The sun shimmered down the paler strands that framed her face, then glinted off the silver stud in her nose. For as long as I'd known and loved Granny Blue, she looked the same way: like a walking, talking rock song.

"You guys already gave me my presents. My new drumsticks and this!" I spun around to model the leather riding vest they'd had made for me. My vest had a white skull-and-crossbones symbol stitched on the back, just the same as Granny Blue's. But above that swanky emblem, they'd asked the shop to spell out my name in rhinestones:

EMMA PEARL CASEY

It was Mama who came up with my middle name. She said my dad named me Emma, after his favorite fictional heroine. But Mama named me Pearl, after her favorite Janis

Joplin album. ("Because I don't want her to tiptoe quietly through her life" is what Mama said when she told me the story. "I want her to scream and sing and howl.") I never knew my dad, but I was happy with the name he gave me. A good name is a fine thing to leave a person.

"So I really don't need another present," I grunted as I tugged the helmet off my head. For the record, my hair did not fall pretty and cascade-y like Blue's. I have tight, curly ringlets that frazzle and point straight to heaven. I call it my hallelujah hair. Not even a helmet can flatten the flouf.

Blue's face was troubled when she looked down at me. She rested her hands on my shoulders. "It's a special gift she's giving you."

"If it's special, why do you look so sad?"

"Honestly, I think the timing is lousy. But your mama disagrees with me, so go on. I'll meet y'all back there."

There wasn't even a hint of joy in Blue's voice. That was true for all of us, for every person who came to the cafe. We all had sadness in our eyes. The day was a celebration, for sure. But even birthdays were dark days back then. Sickness hovered over my mama like a shadow, traced dark circles under her eyes, and pulled her skin tight against her bones.

I found Mama sleeping on the back porch swing with a quilt wrapped around her thin shoulders. We called the back porch our Fortress of Wonder, similar to Superman's

Fortress of Solitude but noisy and fun. We strung Christmas lights all around the beams. We collected nature's treasures and displayed them on old shelves—acorn tops and fossil-rocks and clusters of different-shaped leaves.

I leaned over and kissed Mama's cheek, and she smiled. Even without opening her eyes, she knew it was me.

"There you are," she said, scooting over on the swing and pulling me down beside her. "How was school?"

"Fine," I said quickly, hoping she wouldn't be attuned to the worry in my voice.

Mama tilted up my chin and looked me in the eye. "Those girls giving you problems again?"

A few girls at school had always teased me about my mouth—about the scar that slants sideways from the base of my nose to the tip of my lip. According to them, this gives me a zigzag crooked smile, which they loved to joke about. I tried to ignore them, like Granny Blue suggested. But ignoring them hadn't made them go away. It's almost like it made them even more determined to hurt my feelings.

"I'll be fine," I said, resting my head against Mama's arm.

She played with my hair and hummed a gentle song, the kind that quieted my heart and made me feel safe. We stared straight ahead, at the grassy-hilled slope that bordered our property. The headstones of the cemetery shot up out of the ground like crooked, crumbly teeth. From our back porch, it looked like flecks of glitter hovering around those graves. Of course, I knew I was really just seeing the sun reflecting off the bugs' wings.

But even bug swarms looked pretty when I was beside Mama. Less like pesky insects, more like twilight confetti.

The sun shimmered low over the woods, stretching its warm, orange arms until we felt the light on our faces. Back when Mama felt good, we pressed our hands together and made shadow puppets right there, against the setting sun.

"Emma Pearl," Mama said softly, "I have a gift for you. Blue says you're still too young. But I want to be the one to tell you. You see that old trunk off in the corner?"

"Yes, ma'am." I was already on my feet, walking through that pretty mix of late-day shadow and light. I could tell that the trunk had been one of Mama's gig boxes, from back in the day when she was a touring folksinger. Stickers of some of the cities and countries she'd toured were peeling away from the outside. Worn leather flaps buckled tight around the trunk's bulging middle.

I blew the cobwebs away from the lock. Then I pushed the trunk open. The hinges screamed as loud as one of her electric guitars. The trunk was full of Keeping Susans— which meant something special was tucked inside. Keeping Susans are pale yellow flowers that only bloom in Blackbird

Hollow. We tuck them into letters and old books and boxes of keepsakes, because they help preserve important things.

"Should be right on top," Mama said. "You'll see an old leather book. It's not too big, about the size of a journal. Kinda scuffed up, though."

The book was bound in leather, and secured with a plain black strap. Without even opening it, I could see the edges of hundreds of pages—all yellowed, all tattered and soft, as though dozens of fingers had traced across them. I blew the dust off the cover and studied the faded title.

"'The Book of Days . . .'" I read as I settled in beside Mama.

The book's spine crackled underneath my fingertips when I opened it. It sounded like my spine when I first wake up and stretch in the morning, and I wondered if it was possible for a book to come alive that same way. To tell you things. To change the course of your days.

Blue cleared her throat from the doorway. "Jasmine." She regarded my mama with a worried look in her eyes. "Are you sure this is the best time—?"

"It's fine," Mama said, waving her hand in dismissal. "Come on out here. I want you to be here when Emma hears this."

Blue sighed, but she sat down across from us.

Mama smiled down at me. "For many years, the women in our family have done marvelous and wonderful things.

I'm talking truly extraordinary. Ingrid Noble was the first to write it down. Read the first page, now. See for yourself."

A golden stretch of late-day sunshine fell across Mama and me and the yellowed pages in my lap. My heart felt warm under the weight of the light, but my hands still trembled. I knew I held something special in my arms. I'd seen enough old books to know time turns pages yellow and brittle. Even Keeping Susans can't make a book last forever. The words were faded now, but I could tell they'd been written proudly, and bravely.

I read the words aloud:

Ingrid Noble
The Spy

In the Year of our Lord, 1777, I, Ingrid Elizabeth Noble, became part of the Destiny Dream of my ancestors. On the eve of my seventeenth birthday, I dreamed of the field of blue flowers. Standing in that field was the Great General himself. Thus, I knew my legacy was bound with his somehow.

Shortly thereafter, I entrusted my service to his leadership and began the most terrifying and most wonderful year of my life: I became one of his spies. As a new recruit to the Culper Ring, I personally delivered messages to 711's top officials. I often met with them face-to-face. By day or by night, I'd pull the cloak over my face and make my way casually through the enemy-filled streets.

Some days I walked miles.

Other days, I saddled my horse, Moonbeam, and rode farther still. No one ever even tried to stop me.

After all, who would imagine a young girl with no papers to be a threat?

I am not the first to have the Destiny Dream, but I am the first to write it down. I hope I am not the last. We might be hundreds of years apart. But the thread of destiny connects us all.

This is my admonition to you: History is a story that must be told. And it is up to us to turn the pages.

I shook my head and looked up at Granny Blue. "I don't understand."

Mama tapped the page. "Since before the Revolutionary War, every woman in our family has dreamed of a field of blue flowers. We've kept a record of it since Ingrid Noble. And in that field, they always see . . . a clue. A clue to their extraordinary destiny."

"Did you dream of blue flowers?"

She nodded. "Absolutely."

"What did you see?"

"An electric guitar." Mama grinned. "When I dreamed

of the guitar, I knew I was born to make music that'd shake the world."

"And you?" I looked at Granny Blue. "You had the dream, too?"

Blue sighed. "Your mother and I feel differently about the Book of Days. I think it's poppycock."

Mama laughed. "Your granny Blue did have the dream, Emma. But she got frustrated and ripped her page out. She won't tell a soul what it said."

Blue waved the notion away. "It didn't work for me. That's all. It seems to work fine for most everybody else."

"And Ingrid"—I glanced down at the pages again— "saw a general?"

Mama's eyes flashed excitedly. "Not just *any* general. She saw General George Washington himself." Mama leaned closer to whisper, "She became one of his spies."

Goose bumps rippled up my arms as Mama reached over and turned the page. On the back of Ingrid's note was a newspaper clipping.

"And there's more," Mama said. "Many, many more . . ."

I saw more names, newspaper clippings, letters, and odd trinkets. "We call the women in our family the Wildflowers. Because no matter how difficult the circumstance, and no matter where the wind carried them, they bloomed, bold and bright."

"And I'll be one of them someday?" I asked. I looked to Mama. And then to Blue. "I'll be a Wildflower and do something extraordinary?"

"You better believe it," Mama said softly. *Proudly.* "The women in our family, they have a certain . . . charisma . . ."

My heart fell flat. I did not have charisma.

"A certain . . . grace."

I sighed. I was not graceful, as evidenced by the mustard splotch on my T-shirt. Ever since lunch, I'd smelled like a corn dog.

"The Wildflowers accomplish great things," Mama said. "I'm part of it. And so are you."

I swallowed down the lump of fear in my throat. "Why are you telling me this now?"

"Jasmine." Blue's voice was sharp. "Don't get carried away."

But Mama ignored Blue. "I'm telling you now"—her lip trembled—"because I believe you'll have the Destiny Dream early, Emma. I think it's going to happen for you soon. Often in our darkest days, in our hardest times . . . that's when we find our destiny. You'll have your dream, too. You'll be the youngest Wildflower yet."

"Jasmine," Blue breathed.

Mama held up a weak hand. She looked into my eyes. "I know it's been a tough year for you. And it might be a tougher year for you still. But no matter what happens, you have the dream to look forward to. And then we're connected forever, you and me."

Mama tilted my chin up until I was looking into her eyes, eyes the same color as mine. "You are special to me. You always have been. Never doubt your starry aim, Emma Pearl Casey." She pressed a quick kiss on the top of my head and hugged me close, like she did when I was a little kid. I held her tightly and wished my love was enough to keep her there—right there with me—forever and always.

She whispered against my hair, "If we're ever apart for a little while, you and me, I want you to know we're connected that way. We have the cafe, and all of our special places. We have our songs. And we have our destiny. You and me—we're Wildflowers."

I took one last look at my mama before I walked inside. Her hair blew gently in the breeze. Her thin face looked golden in the fading light. I knew I would always remember my mama exactly that way, not sick. But shining, brave, and bright. Shining even on her dark days. Shining until the end.

CHAPTER FOUR

More thunder shook me loose from the memory of my mama and the day she gave me the Book of Days. My Destiny Dream was coming soon; my mama said it would.

I wouldn't let her down.

I double-checked the lock on the gate. And I stilled as I heard someone call my name.

"Emmmmmma . . ."

Clearly, my brain was just frazzled by the morning's shenanigans: storms and ghost stories and thoughts about destiny. So I commenced with my walking.

But I heard my name again.

"*Emma.*" Now it was a long, low whisper. "Emma Casey . . . I have something to say to you . . ."

Suddenly, a wild mass of curly hair came flying at me from the general direction of the azalea bush. My best friend, Cody Belle Chitwood, giggled as she threw her arms around my shoulders and squeezed me tight.

"Did I really scare you?" She grinned. "I've never scared you before!"

"My nerves are a mess today," I sighed. I locked my arm through hers as we scampered toward the cafe. "I'm happy you're here, CB. I have stuff to discuss."

"Ditto." Cody Belle nodded. "You go first."

"I was restless last night, in a weird way . . ."

"You had the dream!" Cody Belle yanked me to a stop. Then she hugged me tight, swirling me up off the ground.

"Not yet," I said when she finally let me go again. "But it's going to happen soon. I know it. I'll tell you about it inside."

Cody Belle zoomed ahead of me and opened the door. My BFF is a born runner. The girl can move lickety-split fast. I'd never be able to keep up with her if she didn't slow down for me, but she always does. This past year, Cody Belle went to a different school, due to a stupid zoning law. This is one of the big reasons the past year had been especially rotten. We're still best friends even though we aren't together 24/7.

The cafe was steadily filling up with folks. Mugs clinked against the tables. Happy chatter filled the air. Newspapers were fanned open, all bearing the latest news, which never seemed to be good these days. I picked up an abandoned paper on the table and read the headline:

SO LONG, WAILING WOODS?

STEELE ASSOCIATES BUYS TRACTS OF LAND

ACROSS THE CUMBERLAND GAP

"Warren Steele," I muttered. "Cody, go grab our usual spot. I need to talk to Blue."

"I'll have Boneyard Brew waiting for you." Cody Belle patted my shoulder.

It occurred to me that there are at least three indisputable facts about best friends:

1. They wait for you, and
2. They slow down enough to walk beside you, and
3. They always know when you need hot chocolate.

I scrambled down the hallway to Blue's office. Framed portraits of her favorite singers line the walls.

She calls them her pep squad:

Loretta,

Emmylou,

Reba,

Dolly,

and Ramblin' Rose.

My favorite picture is the framed photo on the end. The woman in that photo is wearing a grin so toothy-big you can't even see her eyes. Daisies are woven into the braids of her hair. That's my mama, Jasmine Casey.

A stray beam of golden light broke through the rain clouds outside and reached through Blue's office windows, lighting that photograph just so. It seemed fitting that my mom should be on a wall of stars, that the sun would be her spotlight. Those portraits were a comforting presence to Granny Blue. They made her feel like a tough old broad, she said. That's not exactly what she said, but I hesitate to repeat her verbatim.

Granny Blue was looking out the window, with her back turned to me. But I could tell by her stance she was in tough-broad mode. Her motorcycle boots were planted wide. Her shiny silver hair was bound in a thick braid down her back. The only thing that looked granny-like about her was her apron. But she hadn't been out of her office, so it wasn't scuffed full of flour dust just yet.

When some people hear the word *granny*, they think of a little old lady with sparkly eyes and a twinkly laugh. My granny Blue is not that way. For one thing, she's not little at all; she's taller than most men I've seen. Years ago, long before I came into the world, Blue was a boxer. If Granny was a musical instrument, she'd be an electric guitar. If she was a flower, she'd be one of the wild yellow roses that grow thick in the Wailing Woods. So pretty you can't look away. So prickly that it's hard to get too close sometimes.

And while most people in the Hollow wear flowers in their hair, or pinned to their shirts, or stuck in their baseball hats (or tucked in their beards), Blue's different. She has flowers tattooed on both arms all the way from her shoulders to her wrists.

So she doesn't really look like other grannies in Blackbird Hollow.

But she loves harder and truer than any person I've ever known. Which makes her the best granny I could possibly hope for.

Uncle Periwinkle sat on the edge of Blue's desk, talking to her in a low voice. Thankfully, Blue doesn't do anything quiet, especially talking. Makes it much easier to eavesdrop.

"You want to know what I think of Warren Steele?" Blue's voice rumbled. "In all honesty? I think he's a good-for-nothing dirtbag."

Blue kept her eyes on the graveyard and the silver sky behind it. "But I don't have any other choice."

"Are you sure about that?" Peri asked.

"Look at this place, Peri." Blue shook her head. "It's all run-down. It ain't worth much to most people. I think I got a fight left in me where it matters—for Topher and Emma. For you and Club Pancake."

Club Pancake is Blue's name for her close friends: Peri; Greta; Greta's dearly departed brother, Jacob; and my grandfather. Blue says true friends turn a bad day into something wonderful faster than a pancake flip. Cody Belle is like that for me; she's a pancake flip of goodness even on a crummy day.

Blue sighed. "But for this place? Sometimes I don't know if the Boneyard's worth my fight. It's just a place. It ain't worth much to most people. Warren will give me more for it than most people could."

"But there's more than land tied up in this place," Peri said. "You have memories here. The kids have spent their whole lives here. So did Jasmine."

Blue shook her head. "But what are the kids going to do when I'm gone? You think they'll be able to keep up this dump?"

"So you're just going to sell, then?" Peri asked as he stood up. "Is that it? You're just closing shop and giving up on Blackbird Hollow like everybody else."

"Not by choice." Blue pointed her finger at his face. Then her arm fell to her side and her voice softened. "But I'll give in . . . maybe. If I have to. Money's not coming in like it used to."

Blue crossed her arms over her chest. The trees slashed back and forth in the wind, like they were trying to get her attention.

"He'll probably tear this place down," Blue said, her breath fogging against the glass. "Turn it into a putt-putt course or subdivision. If I sell it . . ."

"Blue!" I cried, jumping out from my hiding place. "What are you talking about? You can't sell the cafe."

Blue sighed. "How long have you been listening, Emma Pearl?"

"Do you even hear yourself?" I asked, coming to stand in front of her. She towered over me, but I didn't mind. I'd always felt safe in Granny Blue's shadow. "You want to sell our cafe? To idiot Warren Steele?"

"Emma, you've never met Warren." Blue shrugged. "You don't know that he's an idiot."

"You just called him a dirtbag."

"Ha! So you *were* eavesdropping."

I waved my hand. "That's beside the point."

Blue's eyes spoke volumes to me. I can't read people as easy as Topher can, but I knew the look in Blue's eyes:

I'm sorry.

I'm tired.

I don't know what else to do.

"Maybe." I hopped up and sat on Blue's desk and sat pretzel-style. Beside me was a thick contract, which, thankfully, Blue hadn't signed just yet. "If Warren could just see this place . . . he'd know it was something special. Maybe he would invest in it!"

Blue gave me a certain look that translated: *Not a chance.* "As far as I can tell, Warren Steele is motivated by one thing: money. And that's it. He's as rich as they come now, thanks to his knack for buying and selling little bits and pieces of the mountains. As if the mountains belong to anybody. As if anybody has the right to sell off trees and dirt roads and tall pine trees. Either I sell it to him, or enough money had better fall from the sky for us to keep it. We don't have that kind of money, Emma. If he's willing to pay for this run-down dump, maybe I should let him have it."

Granny Blue might as well have been talking another language. I didn't see any sort of run-down dump when I thought of the cafe. I saw shade trees tossing shadows across our little back porch. I saw long walks in the woods and mornings among the graves. I saw wildflowers blooming even in the ditch by the road.

And I thought about how just the promise of this place feels to me. Like when school was the pits and I finally got to climb on the bus. I felt the bump on Station Camp Road and knew I was nearly home, to the Boneyard Cafe.

I was home. And this was the rhythm of my home:

The swish-swish of the tall evergreens.

The squeak of the oven door when the sugar cookies get pulled out.

The screen door slapping shut.

Blue singing Patsy Cline songs while she mixes black-berry muffins.

Home, where I always heard music, sometimes the ban-jos and guitars and twangy lyrics on the jukebox, sometimes people stomping out real tunes on the front porch. And always, every day, just voices of people I loved: Topher and Cody Belle and Club Pancake. And my mama, once upon a time. That's the best part of all: I have memories of my mama in every room. I need those memories.

Periwinkle cleared his throat and patted my shoulder. "I think I'll leave you two alone for a bit," he said, and made his way toward the door. "Let's talk about this before you do anything, Blue."

I hopped off Blue's desk and paced across the floor, the same way she does when she's trying to solve a problem.

"Emma—"

"You can't sell this place," I told Blue, and hoped my voice sounded determined. Fiery. Like I meant what I said. "Not yet. Not to Warren Steele. Sell it to Topher someday, when he's a millionaire fiddle player. He'll take care of it."

The sadness was heavy in Blue's voice when she answered, "Don't know if we can hold out that long."

"Do you remember what Mama said about fear?" I asked. "She said fear is just a flashlight that helps you find your courage."

Blue rested her hand on my shoulder. "Well, she knew a thing or two about courage. That's for sure. She was a brave lady."

"We are all brave ladies," I said. "We're Wildflowers."

I left Blue and met Cody Belle back in the cafe. I told her about Warren, and we talked about different ways to stop him. But nothing really made sense, and by that evening, all I wanted was to be alone with the Book of Days.

I went up to my room and opened to a random page.

Lola Daniels

The Journalist

In my twenty-fifth year, I had the Destiny Dream of my ancestors. There was a part of me that didn't think the dream would happen for me at all. My family adopted me when I was a baby, so deep down I've often wondered if the blue flower dream would find me. Turns out, it most definitely did. As my mom always said, a family is a family no matter how it's stitched together.

When I saw a notebook and camera in the field of blue flowers, I knew I was meant to be a journalist. That would be my destiny. But I couldn't afford to leave Blackbird Hollow yet. How could I find a story worth telling stuck here in the mountains?

Terrified of destiny passing me by, I decided to practice. I took photographs of the people in town, the farms, and the flowers. I developed those pictures in a darkroom my husband built for me near our barn. And after a while . . . something happened. I began to fall in love with this place. I've lived here all my life, but seeing the mountains through a camera lens helped me realize the stories I'd missed. I became passionate about preserving the stories here, about collecting photographs that show what life is like here in the Hollow. My articles and photographs went on to win many awards. But the greatest award I won was never a plaque or trophy; it was knowing I'd devoted my days to sharing stories about real people—real lives—that mattered.

My admonition: You don't have to go looking for stories across the world. You only have to look out your window.

It was almost midnight, and Bear and I sat beside each other on my bed, turning the pages in the Book of Days. Clarification: *I* turned the pages in the book. Bear chewed her paws, mostly oblivious to my situation. She turned a few circles on her favorite pillow, then plopped down and woofed at me while I flipped through the book, turning the pages carefully.

I saw more names, newspaper clippings, letters, and odd trinkets:

a lock of hair bound in a ribbon

a plaid scrap of fabric

a button

a butterfly-shaped broach

Someone had taken the time to write titles underneath each name:

The Spy

The Teacher

The Trapeze Swinger

The Swimmer

The Inventor

The Firefighter

The Actress

I touched the ripped seam of the page that should have belonged to Granny Blue. Two years later, and she still hadn't told me why she'd taken it out.

She wasn't the only one who'd done it, though.

Two of my extraordinary ancestors from the 1800s had also ripped their pages loose, just beneath their names:

Lily Kate Abernathy

Amelia Abernathy

Had they thought the Destiny Dream was silly, the way Blue did? Or had they failed to accomplish their destiny? The thought made my belly ache. I pushed the book away and sighed.

"I need to pound out my thoughts," I told Bear.

And I snatched the drumsticks off my bookshelf.

I sat down in front of my windowsill, but before my performance started, I saluted my poster of Meg White, my most favorite drummer of all time.

When Cody Belle and I were kids, she liked to dress up like a princess and wear a tiara. I wore cherry ChapStick, made drums out of cardboard, and painted them with peppermint stripes, just like Meg. Cody thought I was dressed up like a fairy at first, because my drumsticks were glittery back then. "Are those magic wands?" she asked me.

"Yes," I told her. It's the truth, too. They feel magic to me.

I turned my attention back to the twinkling stars over the graveyard. And I pounded a steady rhythm on the windowsill, which was chipped all over from hundreds of nights of drumming. That night I thought about how it might feel to play on a stage. I'd let my braid down and shake my hair in rhythm to whatever wild beat I drummed up. I would feel the vibrations of the music up and down my arms, and sing along when I felt like it. I wouldn't care what anybody said about my smile or my scars because I would be doing what I loved. I imagined my family all in the front row—Blue and Club Pancake and Topher and Bear. And Mama. I like knowing she's always there, hidden away in my imagination. Kind of like a treasure.

I stopped drumming and stilled the sticks in my lap.

Uncle Peri's voice echoed in my memory:

Beneath the stars of Blackbird Hollow
By the shadow of the ridge
Down a path no man can follow
Lies a treasure someone hid . . .

There was a treasure in my town.

Why hadn't I thought about it earlier? If I found the treasure . . . the Boneyard would be safe from Warren Steele. Safe forever. I scrambled across the floor to my bag, and pulled out the notebook where I'd written Peri's song lyrics.

"What was that rhyme he said first, though?" I asked my dog. "It was something kind of corny . . ."

I pushed my squeaky window open and looked out at the graves. I felt like I was putting on a concert for the dearly departed. Which kind of made me feel like a weirdo. Before I lost my nerve, I tried to sing out Uncle Peri's rhyme:

"I'm pure of heart,
Not filled with hate,
I'll . . ."

I looked back at my dog again. "Something about loot?" I asked. Bear scrunched her nose.

"Ah!" I turned back to the window. "I'll use the loot for something great?"

I almost giggled as I imagined a ghost sounding a buzzer like the kind on a game show. I cleared my throat:

"Oh Conductor,
At your . . . pleasure,
Take me to your wondrous treasure . . ."

CAW CAW!

I startled so hard my drumsticks clattered to the floor.

"You scared me, Penny Lane," I said to the crow nestled in the branches of the tree. Blue'd saved the injured bird from the woods back in the spring, and mended her wing so she could fly again. But Penny Lane likes us so much that she mostly hangs out in the tree. She never strays too far from home.

I waited. And waited. At first, all I heard was the sound of my own breath, the tap of my own brave heart. I looked back from the window at Bear and sighed. "Maybe this is too preposterous?"

Bear blinked like she was contemplating my question. But then the air shifted in the room, and a breeze blew through the window, ruffling the pages of the Book of Days. Bear whimpered and crawled under a pillow.

I stood and peered into the cemetery again, clutching the windowsill. Darkness had covered the graveyard . . .

hiding anybody who might be walking there. And then the song found me.

I felt the song before I heard it, creeping against the back of my neck. And then the air in my bedroom grew thick with music. Someone was singing—a child, maybe. The voice was young and wistful, but strong, too. I couldn't tell if it was a boy or a girl or my own imagination making things up.

"Look close, my dear,
And look again,
There's more to this life
Than beginnings and ends . . ."

I stood tall, despite my trembling legs, and swallowed the lump of fear in my throat.

"H . . . Hello?" I whispered out the window.

The graveyard remained dark and still. A sliver of moonlight peeked out from behind the cloud—a bright smile in the sky. The child's voice sang again, barely more than a whisper in the wind:

"Beneath the stars of Blackbird Hollow
By the shadows of the ridge
Down a path no man can follow
Lies a treasure someone hid . . ."

It was the Conductor's song . . . just as Uncle Peri had described it. But it didn't sound like the voice of an old soldier to me. What I heard definitely sounded like a kid.

I flopped down on the floor and pulled my mud boots over my pj pants. "Stay, Bear," I ordered. My dog whimpered again as I shut the door softly behind me, snuck down the stairs . . . and stepped out into Blackbird Hollow Graveyard at night. All alone.

Or maybe . . . not alone at all.

CHAPTER FIVE

"Um . . . hello? Is somebody there?" My voice wavered as I stepped outside. My hands trembled so hard that my light was shaky. Flashlight-disco across the graves.

I closed my eyes, took a steadying breath, and whispered my mama's words: "Fear is just a flashlight that helps you find your courage." I wondered what she might say if she was there with me. She would see it all as a mighty adventure.

She would remind me that I am born to be a Wildflower. *I will save the cafe . . . no matter what it takes.*

So I stood up tall . . . well, as tall as a tiny person can stand, and cleared my throat and sang:

"I'm pure of heart,
Not filled with hate,
I'll use the loot
For something great!

Oh Conductor,
At your pleasure,
Take me to your wondrous tr—!"

I cut myself off with a gasp as a bony silhouette shot up from behind one of the graves and ran toward the gates. I squealed, flopping down backward against a grave. "Excuse me," I said breathlessly to the stone as I used it to pull myself back up. I directed my flashlight beam straight ahead.

At first, the sight of a real ghost launching out of a grave nearly did me in. I tried to scream . . . but only a squeak came out. My desire to save my home was stronger than my fear, though. And so I launched up off the ground and ran through the cemetery, hot on the heels of my ghostly assailant.

"Pardon me, Adeline Carpetta," I yelled as I jumped over her headstone. I jabbed the flashlight in front of me like a lance, illuminating the path of the running spirit.

"Conductor! Wait! Please don't lead me to certain death!"

The ghost slipped easily through the gate, which makes sense—ghosts being spirit matter and all. But its jacket snagged on one of the spires.

Its . . . jacket? I reached the gate breathless and shined my flashlight into the ghost's face.

A very handsome face belonging to a guy around my age.

I couldn't tell much about him in the darkness, but up close, it was obvious that his face did not look ghostly at all.

"You're . . . real," I said.

He didn't speak. Just blinked at me as though he was terrified. This was possibly due to the fact that I'd just chased him through a graveyard, screaming my guts out.

"What are you doing in my graveyard?" I asked.

He still didn't answer with his mouth. But his eyes answered, in a way. I couldn't tell what color they were, but I could see the sadness hidden there. Even at night. Even with only a flashlight between us.

Finally, he blinked, reached his skinny fingers through the gate, and ripped his hoodie free from the spire. He ran down the road, his sneakers making the faintest swish, swish sound. He was a fast, elegant runner, like Cody Belle.

"I give tours!" I yelled after him. "You should come see it in the daylight, because this place is haunted at night. And I mean haunted with a capital *H*!"

Before I took the time to wonder who I'd just seen . . . and why he was in my graveyard at night . . . the song found me again. It definitely wasn't coming from the kid running ahead of me . . . the song came from behind me. My neck prickled as I turned, slowly, and held the flashlight out over the graves. Nobody was there.

. . . Down a path no man can follow
Lies a treasure someone hid . . .

The song was moving, somehow—toward the woods on the edge of the cemetery. I still didn't see anybody. But it was like the song was calling to me, and I had no choice but to follow.

The music stopped at the edge of the Thicket.

Down the hill slope, nestled in a foggy hollow against the woods, there's a hidden section of the cemetery that's not part of our tour. We call it the Thicket, and it's off-limits for everyone because it's so overgrown with scraggly trees and ivy. Blue doesn't want me to clean it out, because she doesn't want me to get snake bit or skunk sprayed or covered in poison ivy, all of which she believes are abundant there.

But I was certain Blue would understand that this time was different. I had to walk into the Thicket. I had to follow the ghost and find the treasure. It was the only way I could keep Blue from selling our home and all the memories I kept there. I imagined the look on her face when I carried a muddy chest full of gold into her office. And I surged on.

I hummed Uncle Peri's song as I made my way down the hill. Fireflies floated in the high grass around me. They looked like little lanterns, guiding me onward. I heard the sound of leaves flutter over me in the wind. The rush of the pine trees shaking and shivering. I pushed through an opening in the ivy-covered gate surrounding the Thicket, and rested my back against a gnarled old tree.

The cafe is only a quick run away, I reminded myself. I can see the lights from Blue's study.

I am brave. I have a destiny. I will not doubt my—

Snap.

POP.

The sound was unmistakable: footsteps.

Steady footsteps walking through the Thicket.

I slunk down close to the ground.

I turned off the flashlight.

My breath rattled the dead leaves on the ground beneath me.

The moon shimmered through the trees, scattering patches of bone-white light all around me. No person moved among the tree shadows. No person I could see, at least.

But I heard someone coming closer.

Somebody was walking through the Thicket, right toward the tree where I was hiding.

What if the intruder had a friend still hiding out here?

What if I really had upset the ghosts?

The footsteps neared.

Pop. Pop. Pop.

"I will not doubt my starry aim," I barely whispered. "I will. Not. Doubt."

I swallowed hard, and peeked around the tree . . .

But nobody was there.

The sound of footsteps stopped.

The moonlight patches seemed to move together then, until the light was shining in one long, silver path to a tall grave covered in ivy. As I watched, the moonlight caught the flicker of something else. Something . . . like stars. Tiny blue stars all over the grave.

I stood up and took a step toward the starry grave. Then another.

And then I felt a cold hand grab the neck of my hoodie and yank me backward. I screamed, and dropped the flashlight.

Granny Blue held tight to my hoodie, looking down at me with one eyebrow raised. Waiting for me to explain.

"I wanted to take a walk." I shrugged. "Clear my head."

"At midnight?" Blue groaned as she reached to pick up the flashlight. "In the Thicket? How many times have I told you this part of the graveyard is off-limits?"

"People back here want to be remembered, too," I said, leading the way out of the woods. Admittedly, it felt nice to step over the muddy threshold back into the cemetery I already knew and loved.

"Bed," Blue said, pointing to my upstairs room.

I shrugged at Bear when I walked in the door. "I tried," I said.

I looked around my room and thought about how strange it was to go back to normal life after such a night. I'd heard a ghost. I'd seen an intruder . . . which I decided to keep secret for the time being. Blue would never let me near the Thicket again if I told her I'd seen somebody sneaking around out there. I looked at my drumsticks and books and posters and mud boots. I loved my room. I liked all my stuff. But I wanted to get back out there. Not just out there in the graveyard near the treasure. But I wanted to run through the unknown again. There was a feeling I had out there, where my fear melted into something better. Something like courage. I wanted to feel that forever.

Maybe all Wildflowers feel that way. I knew I had it in me then; I could be—I would be—extraordinary.

I slid the Book of Days under my pillow and closed my eyes.

"I won't let her sell it," I whispered, as if Mama were in the room with me. As if she really could lean down and kiss the top of my head like she used to. Like I wanted her to.

Bear cuddled against my chest. It never goes away, but at least the Big Empty feels warm when my dog is around. "Mama told me that I have a marvelous destiny," I said as I snuggled my dog close and drifted off into dreamworld.

And my mama was right.

That night I, Emma Pearl Casey, had the blue flower dream of my ancestors.

And it was totally, completely bonkers.

Emma Pearl

The ????

I, Emma Pearl Casey, just had the great Destiny Dream of my beloved ancestors. And I'm writing all of this in pencil, because it makes no sense at all.

Like, NONE.

So. I was standing in my field of blue flowers. And I walked around looking for something obvious and awesome. As I'm looking, I tripped over something on the ground. I look down and see a little burst of different-colored flowers: daisies, violets, and red roses. And in that little burst of flowers . . . I see an old key.

That's it.

An old key.

What?!?!?!

CHAPTER SIX

I always thought the morning after my Destiny Dream would be the best morning of my life.

Like Christmas morning times one thousand.

Like the feeling I have when I wake up on the last day of school times infinity.

But all I felt was confused and nauseous, because my Destiny Dream made no sense.

I couldn't talk to Blue about it. First, Blue thought the Destiny Dream was silly anyway. Second, she was still mad at me for going into the Thicket. I couldn't tell Topher because the boy was still in a baking frenzy. And Cody Belle still hadn't come to the cafe.

That whole morning, I was even more skittish than Bearclaw in a storm.

When the toaster popped and launched burnt bread onto Topher's waiting plate, I jumped. When the oven door squeaked, I squealed. When Topher called my name, I nearly screamed.

"You sure you're okay?" my brother asked.

I gave him a thumbs-up and said, "Peachy."

I'd never said "peachy" before. Is it possible to be so nervous your brain coughs up words you didn't even know it'd stored?

While I waited to pull the muffins out of the oven, I called Cody Belle's house from the cafe phone. No answer.

Blue and Topher kept me busy in the kitchen all morning. It was jamboree day, so the crowd only got thicker as the day wore on. The place was packed. The rocking chairs on the front porch were full. The oven door was in a constant state of squeak as pans of muffins, trays of cookies, and fresh-baked scones were pulled out.

I took a break to referee a checkers tournament, and that's when I finally saw my best friend parking her bicycle against a tree outside.

I grabbed Cody Belle's arm as soon as she walked through the door, and tugged her to the window booth in the far corner. And I told her about my dream.

"You had your Destiny Dream!" She threw herself across the table to hug me.

"*Shh,*" I cautioned. But I nodded and smiled. "Yes, I had it. But it doesn't . . . make any sense! A daisy. A rose. A violet. And a key?!"

Cody Belle scrunched her eyebrows together. "Like . . . a car key?"

"More like an old key," I said. "A skeleton key. Give me your notebook."

I snatched the paper from Cody Belle and drew a picture. "It looked better than that, obviously. I'm not much of an artist. But it was a key. And the key was on a bundle of flowers—roses, violets, daisies." I turned to the window. Blue'd stuck a handful of daisies in a Mason jar and put it on the sill. The daisies were thump-thumping their white crowns against the window, probably because the air vent was blowing on them. But it looked like they wanted to be outside, caught up in the whirling wind.

"Aunt Greta says daisies are a symbol of friendship," I said, more to myself than Cody Belle. I plucked a daisy from the vase and stuck it behind my ear. It's the flower I wear most, because it was my mama's favorite.

Cody Belle shrugged. "Maybe you're supposed to become a florist, like your aunt Greta? Or a locksmith-florist?"

"I don't think so," I sighed. "It'll become clear in time, I guess. It did for the other Wildflowers."

We both stared out the window, toward the Wailing Woods. The rain clouds hadn't burst just yet, but they stretched like a silver warning overhead. It was a spooky, lovely day. Slick green leaves tumbled through the cemetery.

I thought again about my crazy night. I wanted to tell Cody Belle but there wasn't time just then, because it was late afternoon. And that meant it was time for the Boneyard jamboree.

Topher's band, Dogwood Foxtrot, was already set up near the front of the room. Topher tuned his violin while our town librarian, Alice, lit the tall candles situated behind them. Lighting the candles meant they'd start out with a slow set, maybe a few old, haunting ballads that'd roll out into feisty dancing songs.

The candles sparkled directly underneath the large stained-glass window that's been in place since back when the cafe was a church. The window is pieced together with hundreds of multicolored glass shards, all connected to form the image of an old, bearded man. He's raising his arms toward the sky, toward a flock of long-winged black-birds. When the candles flicker and the glass catches the light, all those wings look like they're fluttering. Like they might fly right off the window and into the sky, where they can scrape the stars with their glassy beaks. That window is one of my favorite things about the Boneyard Cafe. Some people think the picture is too sad, but I like it. I like to imagine those blackbirds are kind, like Penny Lane. Maybe they offered to take all the man's sorrows and carry them a million miles away. After the ballads, the band breaks out the fast songs. Those are my favorites.

At least, they used to be. I don't really dance on jamboree nights anymore. I just don't feel right, dancing without Mama. I would rather watch, and remember.

After helping stir and bake and deliver orders to tables, I took a Brew Break with Cody Belle. "The Destiny Dream really has you wound up, doesn't it?" Cody Belle observed. "You know how I know? Because there's nothing in this world much sadder than cold hot cocoa."

I stared into the depths of the mug-gone-cold in front of me. Truly, this was a travesty. This batch of Boneyard Brew was warm and creamy with a heart-shaped marshmallow floating on top. And it's not just the taste of the stuff that's so divine; it's the way it makes people feel. Just one sip can calm a person's nerves in a way that seems almost magical. Blue says it's the secret ingredient. Of course, she won't tell anybody exactly what that ingredient is. Not even me. You have to put in your time doing dishes and mopping floors before you get promoted to Brew Duty.

"I'm going to help you figure out the dream, Emma," Cody Belle assured me. Her forehead scrunched, the way it does when she's trying to remember something important. "Oh! I almost forgot to tell you something: Earl Chance is back in town."

This sudden change of such an important topic might seem strange to those who don't know my BFF. But Cody Belle's brain bounces around like a ping-pong ball. I just try to keep up.

I shrugged my shoulders. "Who?"

"You remember Earl Chance!" Cody Belle nudged my knee with her sneaker toe. "He went to school with us all the way to third grade, just in a different class. Beretta Simpson was crazy about him."

"I might remember him," I said. I vaguely remembered standing beside someone named Earl during our Christmas carol sing-along. I *vividly* remembered mixing up the class dance moves we'd learned. I kicked to the side at the wrong time, and sent everybody on my right toppling like dominos. "So he moved back?"

"Yes. And everybody in town's talking about him."

"Why's that?"

"Earl's a little bit famous now. He was on the national news because he—"

Cody stopped talking mid-sentence. She looked past me, toward the front door of the cafe, her eyes going shiny and wide as the quarters in the town fountain. "Oh. My. Gosh."

"What?" I didn't get worked up at first. Cody Belle has a flair for dramatics.

"He's *here*," Cody whispered. "Earl Chance is in the

cafe. He just walked in the door. That's crazy! I just talked about him and he showed up."

"That's not crazy," I said. "This town's tiny. Everybody comes through here eventually. Don't stare at him." But then I leaned toward her and whispered, "Does he look any different, though?"

Cody shook her head. "No. He's still cute. Really cute."

I rolled my eyes. First, because Cody Belle embarrasses me when she talks about guys that way. Cody Belle herself isn't embarrassed over anything. She just flat-out says what she thinks and feels. I don't think I'll ever be that brave. Second, because of course he was cute. Beretta Simpson only surrounds herself with people who know how to play sports or know how to be attractive. Ideally, her friends must do both things well.

"We need to talk to him," I said, pointing to the flower in my hair. "Daisy Brigade, activate!"

Back when Cody Belle and I went to the same school, we formed a secret club called the Daisy Brigade. In an effort to thwart all the crummy rudeness Beretta and her friends sent out into the world, we decided to make friends with anybody and everybody who felt alone. Admittedly, lots of people don't want to be friends with a graveyard girl. But I still want people to know they never have to sit alone in the cafeteria, not if they don't want to.

"Daisy Brigade, activate!" Cody repeated. "Let's go meet Earl."

I sighed and twisted around.

And my heart pounded out a frantic, fearful rhythm.

I had seen Earl Chance before.

I'd seen him just last night . . . in the Blackbird Hollow Cemetery.

CHAPTER SEVEN

I could barely breathe as I watched Earl Chance saunter toward the counter beside a woman I figured was his mother. She kept her hand on his shoulder the whole time, and leaned into him as she walked, as if her presence alone could protect him from anything. And Earl did indeed look mostly normal: He wore sneakers, jeans, and a Superman T-shirt. And, okay, he was really cute.

By the light of day, he didn't look ghostly at all.

He glanced in my direction, and I reacted in the most obvious way: I slid underneath the table.

To hide.

"Gah!" I yelped as I looked up to see Cody's face two inches from mine. Cody Belle is gloriously tall, which gives her plenty of cool opportunities in life. I've seen her run across the soccer field in six strides. But right at that moment, she looked like a human paper clip all scrunched up under the table. I'm small enough to fit easily into tight spaces. I consider this the Lord's way of making sure the dork species survives.

Cody Belle narrowed her eyes, studying my expression. "This is not effective, Emma. It's Earl Chance. What's the big deal? What happened to the Daisy Brigade?"

"You were right," I said. "I have seen him." And I proceeded to tell her about how we just happened to run into each other while I was chasing a ghost through the graveyard.

"This is so embarrassing," I said. "He'll think I'm an idiot."

Cody Belle scrunched up her face. "I don't know why you care so much about what people think."

I pressed my hand over the holes drilled into the old floorboards. Years ago somebody'd drilled a constellation of holes into the far corners of the room. It was Granny Blue who pointed this out to me. Most people in this town don't notice, she said. They're in such a rush to get to the counter and order a fried banana sandwich that they don't even realize they're stepping on stars.

I peeked out from underneath the table again. Earl and his mom stood at the counter, picking out fresh-made apple fritters.

Blue came around the counter with the bag of fritters and smiled down at Earl. "Do you remember my granddaughter, Emma? She's about your age, I'll bet. She's right over—"

I ducked back under the table before she pointed me out.

"Cody Belle, he's going to recognize me and he's going to tell Blue I chased him through the graveyard."

Cody Belle shook her head. "He definitely won't do that."

"How do you know?"

"He doesn't talk anymore," Cody Belle said. "That's what I've been trying to tell you. He talked when he was here. But Earl survived the tornadoes that tore through the area last spring. People call him the miracle kid. His home, all the homes around him, even a barn and some trees, were flattened by the tornado. But Earl survived. He hasn't talked since."

"Get ready to dance, Blackbird Hollow!" yelled Alice as she pulled her guitar up over her heart. "The sun'll set soon, but we'll kick up some stardust when it does." She nodded at Topher. Topher widened his stance and tucked his violin beneath his chin. His bow sparkled when he twirled it in the air. He pulled it slow and steady across the strings.

At the sound of that first, long note, the small crowd in the cafe let out a happy "Whoop!"

Folks who'd been propped against the corners ran out into the middle of the floor. A group of little kids clasped their hands together and circled up near the center.

Everybody in Blackbird Hollow knows this song. It's called "Darlin' Daisy," and it might sound like any old folk song you come across in the mountains. But this song is special; it belongs to us. It's so old, nobody even remembers when it started.

Topher sliced his bow through the air, pressing an easy scream out of his violin. Alice stomped her boot heel against the beamed floor and sang out the first, familiar lyric:

"Darlin' Daisy, lace your boots up,
Take the lantern, shine it bright,
Oh, these summer days are dwindling,
But we're going to dance tonight!"

Cody Belle and I crawled out from under the table and just dodged a couple swinging around the corner. We stood back against the wall, hoping the commotion of the dance might give us some cover to get a better look at my graveyard assailant. Earl Chance and his mom watched the dancing from the counter. Earl sipped some Boneyard Brew.

"We need to talk to him," Cody Belle said. "It's rude just to stare."

I shook my head. "I'm too embarrassed."

The song tempo began to speed up. I saw Aunt Greta sipping Boneyard Brew in the corner of the room. She didn't wheel out on the dance floor, and she didn't crack a grin. But even she couldn't help but tap her toes.

"Do-si-do through the windy forest,
Write your name on the tall oak tree,
Catch a little star,
Put it in your pocket,
But don't forget to wait for me."

Alice stomped her heel harder against the worn-out floors and shook her hips. The candlelight flickered happily against the stained-glass window. The tempo sped up as folks reached out for one another, arm in arm, hand in hand, swirling around the floors.

If God had a stethoscope, and if He held it up to this part of the dreary world to check for a heartbeat, I hope these are the sounds He'd hear: The sound of boots stomping rhythms out of the dust. The sounds of happy squeals and laughter when people spin out, nearly dizzy from joy. The sound of a scratchy voice, a thumping guitar, a plucky violin. That's what pure joy sounds like.

Sometimes that's when I miss my mama most. Not just when I'm sad, but when I'm happy . . . and I can't share that happiness with her.

"Darlin' Daisy, pass the schoolhouse,
Creep as quiet as a mouse,
Sneak down Dutch and Vine and Main Streets,

All the way to the old church house.

Sing—

"HALLELUJAH!" The crowd shouted, clapped once, then carried on dancing.

The happiness in the room was so thick when people sang and danced, but I could almost feel my heart breaking. If I'd found the treasure the night before, we'd all be fine. We'd be safe. And we would have this perfect little dancing place forever. But I hadn't found it. And if I didn't . . . it's not just my home I'll lose. This place I love, that keeps my whole town bound together, will be gone.

I saw Earl's mom lean down and whisper in his ear. They walked toward the door together, her hand steady on his shoulder. But just before Earl stepped through the door, he paused, still as a statue. He shivered.

And so did I.

Here in Blackbird Hollow, there's a phenomenon that everybody experiences at least once.

Folks call it the Touch.

It's like a light breeze that finds you anywhere—outside sometimes, but often in rooms with no windows or doors propped open. Suddenly, you feel . . . tingly, as though someone walked by and brushed their fingertips across the back of your neck.

Some people think the ghosts are responsible. Maybe you accidentally stepped in a spirit's invisible space. Maybe you crushed his foggy toe. So the ghost whispers, "Boo," down the back of your neck.

Others say it means an angel is close by; it's the air you feel from their wings trembling against the wind.

Some think it's the prayer of a loved one, whispered over you from the Great Beyond.

Some people think it's made-up nonsense. Granny Blue believes it's something only mountain people understand. She says it's the way of the woods and the trees, breathing deep, just taking a moment to be grateful for being alive. She says it's the mountains' way of saying, *Pay attention here.*

Earl touched the back of his neck, too, trying to brush the tingly feeling away. And then he turned his head and looked right at me with his dark, lonesome eyes.

Heat bloomed across my cheekbones but I didn't turn away. I smiled at him. Or tried to, at least. Without realizing I'd even done it, I lifted my hand to cover the scar over my mouth. I guess that meant most of my smile was covered, too.

Cody Belle slapped my hand away. "Quit doing that."

Earl didn't smile back at us. He just stared.

I don't know if it was the fiddle music, the flower in my

hair, or the Destiny Dream that gave me courage. But something did, and I stepped toward Earl Chance.

"Oh, sweet Daisy, don't go fearing,
When we dance along the ridge,
All the ghosts around are friendly . . .
. . . Unless you try to dig!
In the buggy, Darlin' Daisy,
Now ride faster!
None can follow!
Look back once over your shoulderrrrr . . .
Wave good-bye to Blackbird Hollow!"

Just as folks began to hoot and applaud, the front doors of the cafe burst open. A mighty gust of wind howled through the room. The big lights flickered, and then went out. The candlelight fluttered madly against the wind, but extinguished . . . drowning the room in semidarkness. The stormy gray light coming through the windows didn't illuminate much.

A mug of Boneyard Brew hit the floor, shattering somewhere close to me.

Dancing partners squealed and clung to each other, as if the wind might blow them away.

"What in the world?!" Aunt Greta hollered.

"Everybody relax!" Blue yelled over the sound of the wind. She stepped out onto the dance floor, shining her flashlight around, patting people's arms in reassurance. "Everybody be calm."

But the wind tunneled through the room again, howling louder this time. Another shimmering crash, and I heard a terrifying sound . . . like something between a scream and a moan.

I was close enough to Earl Chance to know the sound had come from him, so I jumped for him. The room was dark, but I reached out and found him kneeling on the floor. He was trembling all over, and he kept his hands pressed tight over his ears.

"It's okay," I yelled just loud enough for him to hear me. "It's just the wind."

"Is everybody all right?" Blue called, swirling the flashlight toward us, as the wind finally began to die down. "Who screamed?"

"It was me," I said, even though it was Earl. I just thought he might be embarrassed if folks knew it was him. Everybody already knows I'm nuts. "The wind sound scared me."

Earl's mom leaned on his other side now, looking at him with concern. He dropped his hands from his ears, but kept his eyes on the ground. His cup of brew lay spilled and splattered across the floor. Even with people all around him, Earl seemed so alone.

"Ugh!" Uncle Periwinkle hollered. "Is that bugs I feel? What *is* this?"

The lights came back up.

Cody Belle's gasp broke me out of my Earl Chance trance. I stood and walked toward the window, where everybody was turning their attention.

The clouds still drooped big-bellied and heavy over the hills, but it wasn't the storm holding our gazes just then.

Red rose petals were falling all around the cafe, as thick as rain. They blew past the windows and across the front porch. They caught in the tangle of ivy around the cemetery gate, like little prickles of blood. They fluttered past the treetops. They freckled the stormy skies.

They blew through the open door, scattering across the old wood beams, catching in our hair and tickling our noses.

Blue walked toward the doorway, her eyes on the dark skies. "It's true, then," she said, plucking a petal from her white hair and pressing it between her fingers. "It's a Gypsy Rose summer."

"What is that?" I asked.

It was Aunt Greta who answered, of course. "Only happens every so often. It's been years since the last one. When the Gypsy Roses blow through town, it means—"

"It means the ghosts are trying to get our attention," Uncle Periwinkle said softly.

Earl Chance said nothing as his mom helped him up. He stared down at the rose petals stuck to his hand. He opened his fingers wide and watched the petals fall like ruby rain.

"C'mon, Earl," I heard his mom whisper as she led him out the door.

"Be right back," I whispered to Cody. I scampered to the kitchen and filled a to-go cup full of Boneyard Brew. Then I pushed my way through the chattering crowd and ran outside.

"Earl!" I yelled.

He and his mom both stopped and waited for me to catch up with them. Earl's mom patted him on the shoulder. "I'll wait in the car."

It occurred to me then that I should have pulled Cody Belle outside with me. She's a natural at small talk. I'm not particularly good at any kind of talk.

"I'm Emma," I said to him. "We met last night. I chased you through the graveyard. I didn't want you to leave, necessarily. I just hoped you were a ghost. It's sort of a life goal of mine to see one."

Earl only blinked at me, as if I was the most outstanding freak show he'd seen in his short life.

He had big, pretty eyes, so dark I couldn't really tell

if they were brown or black. *His eyes are dark as ink*, I thought. Full of stories.

"I have a dog named Bearclaw." I blurted my first interesting fact. "She's only two pounds. You have a pet?"

Earl nodded. But he provided no further information.

"I give tours here of the cemetery," I tried next, since that was my second most interesting fact. "You should come! Tours are always free. And you get a cookie when you take the tour. That's part of our incentive package. Plus, there's plenty more to see by the light of day. Night's the worst time to be in the graveyard. The Conductor haunts the place."

Earl shifted back and forth, all fidgety-uncomfortable like he wanted to bolt. He focused on the ground. I'd been ignored enough in my short life to know that was the universal sign for *Leave me alone.*

Maybe if I'd had more time to think, I'd have chosen different words to say. Or maybe if I actually was interesting, and not just strange, I could have made the chitchat easier.

"I'm not good at small talk," I told him with a gulp. "I hear you're not good at it, either. You can walk away, if you want. That's fine with me. But you can come here anytime you want. Most of the ghosts out in the graveyard are friendly. They like to be remembered."

He didn't walk away, so I kept talking.

"And I don't think it's silly," I whispered, lower. "To be afraid of storms. I mean, I'm afraid of sixth grade. And that's probably way sillier than being afraid of a storm. And I'm afraid of people leaving me. That's probably a common side effect of living in a graveyard. But I think of it pretty often, what happens when people . . . leave. I don't know why I'm telling you that."

The storm clouds had drifted away to reveal the setting sun. I stared down at our shadows on the ground and realized grief feels exactly that way sometimes, like a flat shadow. Because I can't kick it off. Because I always see it beside me, behind me, in front of me. I hate the way it sticks right with me.

I shook out of my sad memories and concentrated on the task at hand: small talk. I searched through my brain for an interesting fact about myself. "Oh! Earl!"

I waited until he caved and glanced at me, reluctantly. I smiled. "I'm allergic to furniture polish."

Earl sighed and ducked his head. But I thought I saw the dimple on his face go deeper, the beginning of a smile.

I pulled the daisy from my braid and handed it to him, along with the Boneyard Brew. "Daisies mean 'I'm happy to be your friend.' And I am happy to be your friend if you ever need one. Welcome home to Blackbird Hollow."

I held out the hot cocoa and the flower and I thought he might walk off without taking either, at first. Is it stupid to give a boy hot chocolate and a flower? I felt the familiar flush of embarrassment rising up on my face. But then Earl reached for both. His fingertips just brushed mine when he took the paper cup, and I shivered as if I'd been shocked by static electricity.

I watched Earl walk away. He looked back just before he opened the car door. And I thought I could see another smile—or at least the beginning of one—somewhere in those lonesome eyes.

CHAPTER EIGHT

I woke up early the next morning to the sound of the kitchen ghost making noise downstairs. As usual, the ghost had vanished by the time I got there. My first hypothesis: The ghost was shy.

Actual outcome: Club Pancake was responsible for making the racket.

To their credit, their racket was more of a low mumble. They all sat around one of the tables in the dining room. Each of them had a mug of Boneyard Brew in front of them. Every mug was at a different level of fullness, or emptiness, too, I guess, depending on the kind of day you're having.

Uncle Periwinkle was wearing the same concerned expression he'd had in Blue's office the day before. He flipped through the contract, which was still, thankfully, without Blue's signature. "I still don't think you should sell until we talk more about it, Blue."

"And neither do the ghosts," Greta chortled. "You know

what old people say, Blue. When the roses blow through town, that's the ghosts trying to get our attention for some reason."

"What old people?" asked Granny Blue. "We are the old people now. Maybe the ghosts want us to know it's okay to let it go. To move on."

I eased down on the step, carefully so it wouldn't squeak and give away my spot. I didn't sit because I was tired but because my heart was heavy all of a sudden. Weighing me down.

I looked down at the tiny circle of Club Pancake—heads of silver-white hair all gleaming in the lamplight—and thought about how many friends they'd lost.

The human heart is a big thumping miracle, I decided. What else in the world could keep beating after being so broken?

Periwinkle cleared his throat. "Maybe the ghosts want us to remember that everything wonderful is possible."

Granny Blue smiled. "That sounds like something Emma would say."

"Speaking of Miss Emma." Peri pulled the violet from his beard and twirled it in his fingertips. "I had a happy memory today, on account of her."

Granny Blue smiled fondly. "What'd my Emma do?" I felt my heart thrill at those words. I loved when she called me *her* Emma.

"She was asking about the Conductor's treasure," Peri said.

"Why was she asking about that?" Blue asked. I heard fire in her voice.

"Easy, Blue. I told her we went looking for it when we were kids. That's all. She'd never heard that story before."

Blue shook her head. "Don't tell her any more than that. Don't put any ideas in her head. I don't want her looking for it. Some people never came back when they went after that treasure."

"It's true it drove many good folks crazy," Peri admitted. "But we had fun when we were kids. It was a Gypsy Rose summer that year, too. Remember?"

Blue smiled. "I remember you trembling when you serenaded the Conductor in the graveyard."

"You're laughing now." Peri smiled. "But you weren't laughing then. The Conductor answered us, remember? Don't give me that look, Blue. I know you heard him, too."

Uncle Peri tapped his hand against the table:

"Beneath the stars of Blackbird Hollow
By the shadows of the ridge
Down a path no man can follow
Lies a treasure someone hid . . ."

I shivered. Maybe Blue didn't remember the Conductor's song, but I did. That song—that exact same song—had pulled me into the Thicket.

Peri laughed. "Jacob and I snuck out many nights after that. *Beneath the stars . . .* We figured that meant we could only find the treasure at night, maybe. And *by the shadow of the ridge*—maybe that means it's not too far from the cafe here. The Boneyard sits on the highest ridge in the county. So we took our flashlights and dug so many holes in those woods that it's a wonder one of us didn't fall in and get stuck."

Peri kept talking, but my mind had wandered down a different pathway:

Beneath the stars of Blackbird Hollow.

I'd seen starry blooms on the old grave in the Thicket on the night of my dream. I'd only been looking for clues, but had the Conductor led me right to the treasure?

Down a path no man can follow.

The moonlight had made a path for me, right to that ivy-covered grave. Could it be that simple?

The Touch settled low at the back of my neck. I shivered so hard I nearly made the step squeak.

I would save the Boneyard Cafe. *And* I would complete my marvelous destiny. All at the same time.

The Big Empty would fill back up, because I would feel

connected to my mama forever. It should have been obvious to me all along: I'd dreamed of an old key.

And what does an old key open? A treasure.

My confusing dream suddenly came into focus. My Destiny was clear: I was meant to find the Conductor's riches.

All of the Wildflowers had an extraordinary destiny. Ingrid helped General George Washington. Mama wrote songs that gave people heaps of hope and heart. And my destiny? I would save my town's heartbeat—the Boneyard Cafe.

But before I could do anything else, I needed to sneak back into the creepy Thicket and get a better look at that grave with the stars.

This time, I wasn't going alone.

CHAPTER NINE

It was time to call in reinforcements.

Specifically: I needed Cody Belle. I was fairly certain the ghost wanted me to find the treasure. But trying to track down a ghost isn't the sort of thing you want to do on your own.

Problem: Cody Belle believes there is no such thing as a friendly ghost. She won't even go on my graveyard tours. So this might take some convincing.

Before the sun came up, I was on my bike, zooming toward Cody Belle's trailer. I wanted to take Leatherwood Road, because the pavement was silvery-looking from the night's rain, glassy and studded by hundreds of tiny green leaves. Plus, I love the sound my bicycle makes when it swishes through a puddle. But I'm only allowed on that particular road when I ride with Topher.

So for this journey, Blue said I could still go, as long as I cut the safe path . . . through the Wailing Woods.

"Stay away from the Thicket," Blue said. "Stick to the path through the woods."

"Those woods are haunted, too, you know," I informed her. "You must be confident the ghosts won't mess with me."

Blue just rolled her eyes at me. She put a bag of raspberry muffins in my bag for Cody Belle and her parents and then pushed me on out the door. "You'll be fine."

Most people think the Wailing Woods are a spooky place at night. I have confirmed that much with my own explorations. I'm here to tell you, they are no less creepy by the light of day. Even the sunlight never gets rid of all those shadows. Still, the Sweet Peaches Trailer Park is less than a mile from me, if you cut through the woods. I happily avoided the Thicket, focusing my eyes straight ahead as I zoomed over the ground. I hoped my bike wouldn't plunk in a mudhole that'd send me sprawling across the woods.

I sang my favorite White Stripes song as I rode, just loud enough that I could still hear sweet whistles from the morning birds in the branches. I whistled, too, out of sheer J-O-Y at my circumstances. I was so close to finding the treasure. And I figured the odds were in my favor. After all, the Conductor knew I was pure of heart and just wanted to save my home. All I had to do was find the thing.

Cody Belle lives with her parents in the first trailer in the lot: a ketchup-red double-wide surrounded by a porch

Topher and I helped them build. Green plastic pots of yellow blooms hung from the porch's eves. A thick hedge of confetti-colored pansies surrounded the base of the trailer, too. I've always liked pansies. Greta said a pansy means *loving thoughts*. That's what makes them a perfect border for a home. Especially a home like Cody Belle's.

I settled my bike against the side of the trailer, careful not to trample the pansies. They looked distinct and happy: little smiling panda bear faces.

I didn't even knock before Cody's mom swung the door open.

"What's wrong?" She pulled me inside and rested her hands on my shoulders. Sunrise is a strange time to go visit your friends, apparently.

"It's all fine," I said. I hadn't time for a braid, so my frazzled hair hung like a curtain over my eyes. "I need to talk to Cody Belle, if that's okay."

She looked a bit suspect, but she gently pushed me toward Cody's room. "Go on and wake her up, then. I'll make you both some breakfast."

"Oh!" I spun around and unzipped my pack. "Granny Blue sent breakfast."

I deposited the muffins and dashed down the narrow hallway. I ran in the room and bounced on Cody Belle's bed. She sat straight up and screamed as if I were a monster poised for attack.

"Stop! It's me!" I said, shaking her just enough so she'd know that I really was me and not a prankster ghost.

Cody blinked at me. Then she craned her neck to check the clock on her nightstand.

"Emma," she said in a gravelly voice. "It is six thirty. In the morning. This is unjustified."

"Destiny waits for no man!" I grabbed her arm to pull her out of bed, but Cody just flopped over on the pillows with an *urph* sound.

"Try to focus, Cody Belle. It's important. I know what my Destiny Dream means! The Conductor's treasure is real. And I'm going to find it. What does an old key open? A treasure!"

I reminded Cody Belle about my journey into the Thicket, but I could tell by the vacant look in her eyes that she did not follow. To say Cody Belle is not a morning person would be a drastic understatement. She pretty much walks in a fog until at least noon.

I leaned in close to Cody Belle. " 'Beneath the stars of Blackbird Hollow' . . . most people hear that, and they think it means they can only find the treasure at night. But it might not be sky stars. The stars might be *in* Blackbird Hollow Cemetery. The treasure might be there, too."

Cody popped her retainer out of her mouth, pulling a long, shiny thread of drool with it. "If you're going to ask me to dig for buried treasure in a cemetery, my answer is NO."

"I would never dig in the cemetery," I said, my voice sounding every bit as hurt as I felt. "Not unless I was a hundred percent sure it was there."

"Emma!"

"It's a lead, Cody Belle. Let's see if there's a name on the stone, and if that person really existed. If they didn't, maybe it's a decoy. Like 'X marks the spot' or something."

"What if we do find the Conductor's treasure?" Cody Belle asked.

"We'll use the loot to save my favorite place on earth!"

Cody Belle blinked at me. "Dollywood?"

"The cafe!" I said, working to keep my voice low. "We'll use the loot to save the cafe. Warren Steele's after it, Cody. When he wants something, he gets it."

Cody Belle frowned. "Lots of people disappeared trying to find that treasure, Emma."

"That's because they had shady intentions," I said. "And after last night, I know the Conductor wants me to find it."

"Or," Cody Belle whispered, "the Conductor knows you want the treasure now . . . and so he will lead you to certain death."

"We'll worry about the particulars later." I patted her leg. "I just need you to come with me. It's my Destiny Dream, Cody Belle. It can't be wrong."

"But why do you need me?" Cody Belle whined.

"Because the Thicket freaks me out. I don't want to go alone again."

Cody Belle flopped backward and pulled her comforter over her face.

"Please?" I pleaded.

"The Thicket is as spooky-creepy as all get-out," Cody Belle mumbled from underneath the covers. "And Blue says you're not allowed there."

"This is different." I flopped down beside Cody Belle. "This is research."

A short silence made me wonder if Cody Belle'd fallen asleep. But then she tossed the comforter back and mumbled, "Fine. I'll go with you."

"You will?" I brightened, bouncing on her bed. "You'll go even though you're scared of the Thicket?"

"Only because I don't want the Conductor to drag you away into the caves or lead you to certain death." She sighed. "I'd never forgive myself if that happened. But why do we have to go so early?"

"Because Blue's busy baking for the day and nobody's at the cafe yet," I whispered. "Which means we can sneak in, investigate, and sneak back out, lickety-split. Just think, we might have the Conductor's treasure before lunch!"

When we ran into the living room, Mrs. Chitwood stood in front of the window, shaking her head slowly. She said nothing. A rain of red rose petals fluttered past the window glass. They fell as thick and soft as snow.

"Gypsy Rose summer," I said. "It means the ghosts are restless."

Mrs. Chitwood nodded. "I was a little girl the first time I saw the roses fall. I remember sitting on the tailgate of my dad's truck downtown. We ate ice-cream cones, side by side. And the rose petals kept falling, falling . . . sticking to our ice cream. Sticking to my eyelashes. And we laughed and flung them away. I miss my dad so much. I don't think the roses have anything to do with ghosts. I think they fall as a reminder that we never lose the ones we love. That they're still watching over us."

Cody Belle wrapped her arms around her mom's waist. And her mom tugged her close and kissed her on top of the head. I felt shot through the heart at the sight of it; I tried to imagine my mama's arms wrapping around me again. But the memory of a hug isn't the same as the real thing.

"Oof!" I squealed as Mrs. Chitwood pulled me in for a hug, too. "Have fun today. Don't get in too much trouble."

Cody Belle and I ran for our bicycles while red petals flurried down all around us.

CHAPTER TEN

The sun was barely awake, floating gently above the far-away mountains. But even summer sunlight can't penetrate the darkness of the Wailing Woods. Cody Belle sighed and clicked her bike helmet in place. "Do we have to cut through here?"

"The Thicket's right up against the boundary of the Wailing Woods. Makes it easy to sneak in. Just think, CB. Someday when we're old like Club Pancake, maybe this will be the story we sit around and tell. 'We found a buried treasure. We saved the cafe. And the graveyard.' We could save the entire town! Besides, we have our Tracking Devices. We'll be fine."

Despite poor cell phone reception in Blackbird Hollow, Blue and Mrs. Chitwood gave us cheap phones last school year, but only for emergency situations. Since the phones are only used to keep tabs on where we are, we call them the Tracking Devices.

"I don't think ghosts are going to be intimidated by the Tracking Devices," Cody Belle said. "I get nervous when I'm in the Wailing Woods. Maybe most of the ghosts in this town are friendly. But something in those woods . . . it makes me nervous. Always has."

I shivered, too. I couldn't help it. But then I shook off the shiver and clicked my own helmet into place. "This time will be different. I can't explain it . . . but I feel like the Conductor trusts me. Trusts us."

The evergreen trees in the Wailing Woods are giants; they've been growing for centuries. They look big enough to scrape the stars. So big that if you walk under them at night, you'll swear the Milky Way looks like a gauzy cobweb spread over the tops. And those trees are always swaying, just slightly. Even when there's no wind that you can feel, you can still see the branches shaking and shivering. The trees in the Wailing Woods are never silent; they always sound like they're whispering secrets to one another.

As we traveled deeper into the shadows, I wondered about those secrets.

I wanted to know what was hidden in those woods.

"I've got you, Emma," Cody Belle said as she boosted me up over the high fence surrounding the Thicket. Cody's legs are so long that she's a natural at fence climbing. She always has to give me a boost. But once I get started, I can spiderscramble across anything.

I swung my leg over the top of the fence, and then jumped down to the other side. My sneakers made a wet thumping *FWOP* sound as they hit the muddy ground.

Cody Belle jumped down next, graceful and catlike.

The birdsong in the trees faded when Cody hit the ground, as if every animal in the woods became alerted to our presence. We were officially within the boundaries of the Thicket now—almost in exactly the same spot where Blue had snatched me by the collar a couple of nights ago and marched me back inside.

"Mama used to say this was a sacred place," I whispered, surprised by how loud my voice sounded in the quiet woods. My voice is never much louder than a ripple, but even small voices sound loud when you talk about things that matter. And I guess that's the most important thing I've learned from giving cemetery tours: Every word you say in a graveyard seems to matter so much. I think about how nobody knows how long they have in the world. And how we only get a certain number of words to say and share. I'd hate for the last words that come out of my mouth to be mean ones. I don't want my words wasted.

"Sacred because it's a final resting-place?" Cody whispered with the slightest tremble in her voice.

"Kind of," I said. "Mama said there are true sacred places in the world. Most of them don't have walls or ceilings, she told me. Sometimes, when you least expect it, you just happen upon a place that feels . . . special. You feel like it was created just for you, to settle your soul. The kind of place you feel as much as you hear or see. She said there are thin places in the world—where you get this feeling like, if you could reach out your hand, you'd touch a whisper-thin veil separating this world from another one. A world you can't even see."

"Like heaven?" Cody whispered.

I fell silent for a moment. "Maybe," I finally answered.

We stood still for a time, long enough for the birds to rest their voices and tune the whistlers in their beaks. Once they started singing again, Cody Belle relaxed beside me and looped her arm through mine.

We ambled through the Thicket. The tree limbs above us looked like skinny arms stretched across the sky— reaching desperately for one another, but never touching. Cody Belle turned on her flashlight and pointed it straight ahead. She kept her shoulders pulled back and her eyes focused on the path in front of us. "Why isn't this place part of the tour?"

"The graves back here are too old. They're fragile. We don't want people accidentally pushing them over or stepping on them. Plus, Blue thinks it's full of snakes and skunks and stuff. She had the gate put up years ago to keep people out."

Cody Belle stiffened.

"We're okay," I assured her. "I'll rescue you from any wild animals."

"I didn't realize the graveyard went this far back."

"Most people don't."

"Do you remember where you were the other night? When you heard . . . him?"

"That's another thing. I'm not sure it was a 'him.'" It was hard to remember what the Conductor sounded like that night. "The voice I heard was softer. More of a whisper. I guess the Conductor's a man, but it was hard to tell."

"Well, where were you standing when you heard . . . it?" Cody asked.

"I can't remember exactly. It was dark. Plus, before last night, I hadn't been back here since I was little."

Cody Belle nudged me with her elbow. "You're still little."

"Even littler, I mean. WHOA! Careful!"

I tugged Cody Belle's arm so she didn't trip over a short,

flat rock jutting up out of the mossy ground. "Watch out for the graves," I whispered.

"There's no way that's a grave!" She leaned down close and looked. "It doesn't even say anything. How do you know it's not just a rock?"

I leaned down beside her and pushed away the cluster of ivy draped across the flat part of the stone. "You can feel a few letters if you trace your finger across the surface. And a little bird design, right up at the top. See? Somebody carved it all in by hand, but it didn't go deep enough to last."

I took up a cluster of dying leaves and dandelions, the best I could do for a bouquet. I twisted a sprig of ivy around the leaves, and settled my bouquet at the base of the little stone. "Blue said some of the first pioneers are buried here, people who came from faraway shores and made their home in Blackbird Hollow."

Cody tucked her arm through mine again. "So. Which way's the starry grave?"

"I don't remember exactly," I said, pausing on the rise of a forested hill. Cody Belle gasped at the sheer number of stones stretched out ahead of us.

"Isn't it beautiful?" I said. "We'll take two different rows, but let's not get too far apart."

We walked around the forest, pausing to look at the old stones.

BEGONIA McINTYRE
1800–1887

SO FAIR AND BRIGHT THROUGHOUT THIS LIFE,
SO FEARLESS AT THE END.
SHE WAS A WIFE. A MOTHER. A SISTER.
A TRUE AND FAITHFUL FRIEND.

HYACINTH McINTYRE
1806–1850

SO FADES THE GLORY OF THE WORLD.

"So fades the glory of the world," I whispered.

Just as my words dissolved into silence, Cody let out a scream so loud and shrill I jumped and fell backward into the mud.

"Cody Belle!" I lunged off the ground and ran toward where she was standing, flapping her arms like a frantic pigeon. When I nearly got there, I tripped over a tree root and slammed into her. We both tumbled to the muddy ground.

"What's wrong?" I said, locking my arms underneath her and pulling back toward the tall tree. "Did you see a ghost?"

"Worse." Cody Belle ruffled her fingers through her hair and shivered. "I walked into a spiderweb."

"Well, I'm pretty sure you scared away any spider within screaming distance."

The Touch came suddenly, a cold pressure on the back of my neck.

"Emma," Cody Belle whispered. She touched the back of her neck.

"You feel it, too?"

She nodded quickly. Then she pointed a shaky finger over my shoulder.

"Look behind you . . ."

Tiny violets bloomed out of the muddy ground, one by one, forming a perfect path to a tall, ivy-covered stone.

Cody Belle sprang up off the ground as if she'd been catapulted. I latched on to her ankle before she ran off. "You said you'd stay with me!"

"Did you see what just happened?"

"Come on. We can do this. We're so close!" Holding on to Cody Belle, I pulled myself up off the ground. We held hands all the way down the violet path.

"This is definitely it!" I whispered as I came down on my knees in front of it. Tiny blue flowers bloomed through the ivy, but they didn't glitter the same way as they had last night. "The moon must have shimmered over the petals a certain way," I told Cody.

"They do look like tiny stars," she said. "I've never seen them before . . ."

Three flowers bloomed among the ivy ropes:

Violets,

White daisies,

And on a short bush, a single red rose.

Just like the flowers in my dreams.

"That's mega-creepy," Cody Belle whispered.

"Help me figure out what the stone says." I pulled the thick tangles of ivy away from the stone facing.

"You still think it's just a fake grave?" Cody Belle asked.

I shrugged. "It's possible!"

Cody Belle and I yanked and pulled at the stubborn ivy. "Emma!" she gasped. Then she reached out to trace a mark on the part of the stone she'd uncovered—a starry mark. "It's not like a Christmas tree star," she said. "It's more like the kind you see on a map."

"A compass rose?" I asked excitedly. I pulled my notebook from my messenger bag and gave it to her. "Until Blue and your mom get us Tracking Devices with a camera, we'll have to make do with your artistic talent. Draw it so we don't forget what it looks like."

While Cody Belle sketched the star, I resumed ivy-tugging duties.

Finally, I found a name. That probably meant it wasn't

a fake stone, so I declared the truth of the situation. "Someone loved you . . . Lily Kate—"

A sudden shiver twizzled down my backbone, so cold I jumped off the ground and gasped. But this kind of cold chill wasn't a bad thing. It felt more like plunging in a swimming pool on a hot day, when you first hit the water and it's so cold it takes your breath away. And then it just takes you in, makes you feel free and happy.

That's how I felt, like I'd discovered something amazing.

"What's wrong?" Cody Belle asked, coming to stand beside me.

"The grave's definitely not fake," I whispered. "I know this name."

I kneeled again, pulling the rest of the ivy away, and thumbed the dirt out of the shape of the name.

Cody Belle read the stone aloud:

LILY KATE ABERNATHY
1845–1860
SHE CARRIED THE LIGHT OF A BRIGHTER WORLD.

"Do you think she was connected to the Conductor?"

"I don't know." I swallowed. "But she does have something to do with me."

"What makes you say that?"

"Lily Kate Abernathy was a Wildflower. She's in the Book of Days," I whispered. "Her name is in the Book of Days, at least. But there's no entry. She's there, but her destiny is not."

CHAPTER ELEVEN

"We're both still shaking," Cody Belle said as we stumbled onto the porch of the Boneyard Cafe.

"We're probably in shock," I reasoned. "Shock manifests in different ways. I've read about the phenomenon, how shock and adrenaline make some people do crazy things. Like, you get your leg bit off by a shark, but suddenly, you're so full of energy and the will to survive that you swim to the shore before you even notice you're bleeding. Maybe we're in survival mode right now. Boneyard Brew will help."

Cody Belle's breathing was quick and choppy, as if she'd just finished a soccer game. Her hands shook as she fished through her rain jacket for a watermelon candy to soothe her nerves. "Let's tell Blue that the Conductor showed you the way to your ancestor's grave. Emma, you need to talk to Blue right now before this gets too weird!"

"It's already weird! I'm not bothering Blue with any of this," I said. "She's already too worried as it is. She's worried about me. She's worried about the cafe. I can solve this problem without her help. It's my destiny."

"She can find professional treasure hunters to take over from here. Let them deal with the ghost." Cody Belle's fingers trembled so badly she couldn't peel the wrapper off her candy. I had to help her.

"Calm down," I said as I pulled Cody Belle into the cafe and hauled her toward the counter. "We need to think. Two mugs of Boneyard Brew!" I called out to Topher. "Quick! We're distressed."

"Distressed over what?" Topher asked as he slid our mugs in front of us. Heart-shaped marshmallows floated on top.

"The mysteries of life," Cody Belle said. Her mug trembled as she raised it high, sloshing brew onto the counter. "Cheers."

Within a sip or two, some of the color returned to her face. "Well, as my dad says, 'Every situation has a sunny side.' At least now we know that the Conductor didn't bury treasure under that star. Your long-lost ancestor is buried there!"

"But there is a star on her grave. And starry flowers. And why's her page just"—I gulped—"gone? I know I heard the Conductor. It led me to Lily Kate Abernathy's grave. And then I dreamed about an old key, which is obviously for opening a treasure chest. Lily Kate has something to do with it. We just have to figure out what."

"You don't know anything about her?"

I shrugged. "Only that she had the Destiny Dream. The rest of her entry was gone." I pulled the Book of Days from my bag and showed Cody Belle.

Cody Belle narrowed her eyes as she studied the entry, tracing the jagged rip of Lily Kate's page. "Do you think it fell out?"

"It looks like she—or somebody—ripped it out."

Cody Belle cocked her head. "Why would she do that?"

"Well, Blue removed hers because she thought the Book of Days and Destiny Dreams were just 'made-up silliness.' She still won't tell me what she dreamed about." I shrugged. "Maybe Lily Kate was that way. Or maybe she didn't fulfill her extraordinary destiny. Maybe she was like me—a klutz-tastical mess."

Cody Belle scowled. "You are not—"

"Maybe," I kept going, "Lily Kate wrote down the blue flower dream as soon as she had it. Maybe she figured she'd fill in the specifics later. But then maybe it didn't work out and she was embarrassed. So then in a mad rage she ripped the entry from the Book of Days and flung it into the fire!"

Cody Belle's lifted mug stilled in midair. "Now who's being dramatic?"

I took a long sip of my brew and shook my head. "At least I'm not my family's first failure."

"You are not a failure!" Cody Belle yelled.

"*Shh.*" Asking Cody Belle to keep her voice down is like asking the Gypsy Roses not to blow. Her voice has one volume, and that is loud, and that's just the way it is. "Once we find the treasure, everything will make sense. I know it."

Topher turned around from the mixer to check on us. I waved.

"What kind of treasure were y'all talking about?" he asked.

He slid a plate of fresh peach-lavender muffins in front of us.

"Uncle Peri mentioned the Conductor's treasure the other day," I told him, peeling off my muffin paper. "We were just discussing it."

"How about you discuss the treasure while you deliver these muffins to table four?" he said with a grin, pushing another basket toward us.

"Somebody ordered a whole basket of your muffins? Snazzy."

Topher beamed. "I'd take them myself but I'm swamped back here."

"Be right back," I told my BFF.

I heard the *ting* of Cody Belle's watermelon candy when she spit it out on the plate. She tore into her muffin. "Take your time. I'm in muffin heaven."

Blue was leaning over the jukebox, staring intensely at the records inside. The glow from the jukebox shone over Blue's face, stitching deep shadow-lines around her eyes. She sighed and pushed a quarter into the slot. Her favorite song, "Ring of Fire," came crackling through the speakers.

"Ring of Fire" was Blue's fight song back when she was a famous boxer. I could picture her bouncing back and forth in the ring, spry and feisty, hair piled high on her head, as she stared down her opponent . . . while Johnny Cash crooned her fight song over the speakers. I think everybody has a song like that, a tune that gets them so revved up you think it's magic. Blue hadn't put on her boxing gloves in years, but "Ring of Fire" still called to the fighter deep within. If the notes had ventured into the air, she might have snatched them, just so she could clutch them tight in her fist.

She was stirred up over something.

She needed to fight now, too, just not with boxing gloves.

I leaned against the jukebox beside her. "What's wrong?"

"Warren Steele's people are coming." Blue shook her head but didn't look at me. "They need to survey the land."

"What?" I shouted. "How long have you known?"

"Emma." Blue looked down at me with sadness in her eyes. "We talked about this."

"Not this, exactly. You didn't tell me he was coming to look at the land today."

"He's probably not coming. His people are, just to get an estimate. I wasn't sure when he'd be here."

Now it was my turn to stare into the glowing jukebox so Blue wouldn't see the frustration—or the determination—on my face. I knew what I was meant to do: I had to figure out what my dearly departed ancestor Lily Kate Abernathy had to do with the Conductor so I could find the treasure and save the cafe. But there was no way I could do all that before Warren Steele's minions showed up. And I didn't like the thought of letting them march around in my graveyard without giving them a piece of my mind.

What would the other Wildflowers have done in a situation like this?

I pondered as Johnny Cash sang to me, then a name came to mind.

"Daphne Prescott," I murmured.

"What?" Blue propped her hand on her hip.

"She was a Wildflower." I'd spent so much time going through the Book of Days lately, I could practically see Daphne's page in my head.

"I know who she was." Blue scrunched her eyebrows at me. "Don't get any crazy ideas, Emma."

"Sometimes crazy ideas are the best ideas, Blue. They're glorious."

Blue patted her hands on my shoulders and turned me toward the dining room. "Deliver those glorious muffins to the young lady reading at the corner table before they get cold."

As it happens, I'd dawdled long enough that someone had already delivered another basket of muffins. Cody Belle sat across from the young lady Blue was referring to: my favorite mountain fairy, Waverly Valentine.

"Every nook and cranny in Blackbird Hollow is haunted," Cody Belle was saying as I made my way to the table. Since Waverly had her own basket of muffins now, I helped myself to a fresh one from the basket in my arms. "Even my neighborhood is haunted. I live in Sweet Peaches Trailer Park. Our ghost, Eli Tucker, used to make up holidays, at least once a week, but sometimes more than that. Wear Your T-shirt Backward Day. Celebrate Alabama Day. Mismatched Sock Day."

"Cody Belle and I still celebrate that one," I told Waverly. Cody Belle swiveled around and kicked out her legs so Waverly could see her fine pairing of stripes and polka dots.

Waverly smiled. "Cool."

"I see you two have met," I said, pulling up a chair.

Cody Belle nodded. "The kitchen had me deliver more muffins because you're too slow. Waverly was walking in the woods this morning when she thought she heard something, so I was just here assuring her that she probably did."

"It's true," I said. "Whole town's haunted. I don't mean to interrupt but we really need to—"

"So as I was saying," Cody Belle carried on. "Eli celebrated birthdays of people he didn't know. Usually famous people—like Willie Nelson and Abraham Lincoln. There's no telling who he'd pick to celebrate. But once he got it in his mind to celebrate something, he set off in his little blue truck for the state line to buy fireworks. And as soon as he got back home, he'd bunch up the fireworks in his scrawny arms, let out a crazy cackle, and take off running through the woods. Sometimes he set off fireworks all night long. Drove most people in the town bananas. But I thought it was fun."

"It didn't drive you bananas?" Waverly asked with a grin. She was wearing dark-rimmed glasses today, with tiny little rhinestone clusters in the corners.

Cody Belle shrugged. "I think it's kind of a cool way to live—to find something to celebrate every day. And it's not like he set them off right beside our trailer or anything. He'd run up into the hills for his fireworks show. I always thought it sounded pretty, like somebody popping popcorn above the clouds. Anyhow, Eli died a few years ago. But people claim that they still hear his fireworks some nights, just that faint poppity-pop-pop in the skies. My grandma says it's a sacred echo. She says it's proof that Eli's still celebrating in the hereafter."

"Well, that's a lovely thought," Waverly said, reaching for a muffin. "I started to head back to the trail this morning and . . . I got a little spooked."

"The ghosts around here are friendly," I assured her. "I mean, the dying part of their lives was tragic. But they lived marvelous stories full of wonder and hope and love . . ."

"Ugh." Waverly peeled the paper off her muffin. "I'd sooner believe in a ghost story than believe in love."

"That doesn't matter," I told her. "Love still believes in you." Even in the most perilous times—like when I'm plotting to save my family's home and business—I'm a hopeless romantic. I can't help it.

Waverly gave me a sad smile.

"We have to go, Cody Belle," I said, pulling my best friend away from the table.

"I am not going to dig," Cody Belle told me in an anxious whisper.

"No digging," I promised. "Not yet."

Cody Belle sighed as she uncapped a bright green marker. We sat on the front porch of the Boneyard Cafe, making protest signs. The air around us was permeated with inky-wet marker smell.

CAW CAW.

"Hey, Penny Lane," Cody Belle said without looking up.

Penny Lane swooped up to the roof of the cafe and perched over us, admiring our work.

"You might be surprised when Penny Lane talks back someday," I said. "Blue always said you could teach a crow to talk."

"That'd be weird but awesome," she said. "So, about Waverly. Do you think somebody broke her heart?"

"Probably," I said, steadying my own marker on the edge of the poster. "My mama used to say said that everybody you meet is a walking, talking broken heart. Some people put the pieces back together better than others."

"That sounds like a song." Cody smiled.

I nodded. "She used to sing it to me. Okay!" I popped the lid back on the marker. "Tell me what you think."

I proudly held up my freshly inked protest poster:

BOO ON YOU, WARREN STEELE!

"Cool." Cody Belle nodded. "Here's mine:

GET AWAY FROM THE RIDGE!

OR I'LL PUT YOUR KEYS IN THE FRIDGE!

"I . . . uh"—I shook my head—"don't know if it makes sense."

Cody Belle shrugged. "I wanted it to sound menacing but not evil. You know?" She pulled the smaller poster boards and started marking them up the same way. "What made you think of a peaceful protest?"

"Daphne Prescott. She's one of the Wildflowers in the Book of Days. Dreamed she was standing in the field of blue flowers, holding a sign that read VOTE in one hand and the American flag in the other. We're not doing something quite that important, obviously. But I think Daphne would approve."

Daphne Prescott
The Suffragette

I am seventy-four years old, and far too close to Glory's gates to have the Destiny Dream of my ancestors. At least, that's what I thought. But I was wrong. Not a week ago, I dreamed of a field of blue flowers. In the field, I saw a mirror.

And in that mirror, I saw myself holding a sign that said WOMEN GET THE VOTE!

In my other hand, I held an American flag. Now, it's a cause I've been passionate about, that's for certain. But it's a cause I've supported quietly, and in my own heart. Who wants to hear a seventy-four-year-old lady talking about women and the vote?

Turns out, lots of people do.

I pinned a yellow rose to my apron. And I campaigned for the vote through the entire Hollow. Folks were surprised

when they saw me. They said I'd never been one for caus-
ing a stir. That's a shame, I've decided. Because there are
things in life worth getting stirred up over. I took the train
to Nashville with women twenty and thirty years younger
than me. But age was no barrier between us, and I felt
younger than I ever had.

We all waited at the capitol building on the day the vote
was taken, all wearing yellow roses on our lapels. Finally,
a young man told us women had the vote . . . by a margin
of one.

My admonition to you: You are never too old to be
daring. Whether fifteen or ninety-five, when the Destiny
Dream finds you, believe your words have power. And
use them.

Cody Belle nodded. "It matters big. Don't worry. You'll
have your entry in there soon. Let's get rid of Warren Steele's
minions and then we'll find the buried treasure."

By the time Warren Steele's survey people showed up at
the Boneyard Cafe, I'd enlisted the Marcums, plus a bevy of
patrons, to help stage a peaceful protest. The surveyor was
surely surprised to pull up in the parking lot and see ten
people with signs, barring the gates of our beloved
graveyard.

It was an old man who climbed out of the truck. His
yellow hard hat and thick white mustache made him look

more like the mayor of a cartoon town than one of Warren Steele's minions. Frankly, as he read the signs we were holding, I couldn't tell if the look on his face was one of approval or amusement. "Care to tell me what this is all about?" he asked, looking first to the adults among our group.

Cody Belle answered, hoisting her menacing-not-mean sign as high as possible. "Back away from the graveyard!" she yelled.

The guy held his hands up in surrender. "I'm just here to survey. I'm not digging up any graves. I've heard the stories all my life, too. I wouldn't mess with the ghosts for anything."

"Survey if you must," I told him. "We'll wait here peacefully. And when you go back to your snake of a boss, Warren Steele, please tell him that we are here to protect this place. No matter what it takes."

"Also, you'll have to climb over the gate to get in," Cody Belle yelled. "Emma's the keeper of the key, and she left the key at the Taco Mart downtown."

"It's true." I nodded. "When somebody puts a plate of nachos in front of me, I lose my train of thought." Of course, he could have just entered the graveyard via the cafe. But I decided to keep that fact a secret. I hoisted the sign up. "Also, *please* be careful in the graveyard. Some of the graves are hundreds of years old."

The man tipped his hat at me and smiled. "I promise to be careful."

I nodded. "Come back for a tour sometime! I give them every—"

"Could we, um, hurry up just a smidge?" Mr. Marcum said kindly. "No offense, Emma. We're just getting hungry over here."

The old man waved to his crew. They were a scrawny band of surveyors, but climbing over or through that gate is no easy task. Between all of them nearly getting stuck as they climbed and my band of peaceful protesters, we drew quite a crowd that day. All summer, I'd taken out weekly tour ads in the *Tailfeather*, our town's only newspaper. They only charged me fifty cents for each ad, but that kind of change adds up. I'm not sure any of my ads ever drew the kind of attention we had then.

Among the throngs of onlookers a newly familiar face showed up: Earl Chance.

"Earl!" I grinned and waved. "Want to help us protest? You don't have to talk. You can just hang out."

Earl didn't speak, of course. But he looked like he might be about to smile. Or even laugh a little bit.

"Welcome back to the Blackbird Hollow Cemetery, Earl Chance!" Cody Belle bellowed.

I kept my sign in front of me, but walked over to where

he stood. His hoodie was unzipped, showing a Batman T-shirt underneath. "There's no tour today, on account of Warren Steele's evil minions surveying the property. Why don't you go inside and grab a free cookie and brew anyway?"

One of the men in the graveyard suddenly yelled, "D'ya hear that, boss?"

I spun around to see the rest of the crew pointing fingers at the woods.

"You've probably made the ghosts mad," Cody Belle said. "They don't like it when people are up to no good in this town. They'll put your *keys* in the *fridge*!"

"It's fine, folks," said the grandpa in the yellow hard hat. "You're a bunch of grown men! Stop acting so skittish."

"Hold on, now . . ." A man in overalls stepped up and pointed shakily. "Aren't those the Wailing Woods?"

I nodded. "They're full of history! A Civil War skirmish happened there! And legend says that ghosts watch over the—"

"I know the legend," the scrawny man in overalls yelled, running for the gate. He was huffing and puffing and red faced when he finally squeezed out through the bars. "I didn't know we were right on the woods. I'm headed home. Warren Steele can survey his own land."

"Ain't nothing to worry about!" yelled the boss in the hard hat. "The ghosts ain't mad unless you hear something . . ."

As if on cue, a faraway sound—something like a high-pitched, wheezing squeak—echoed throughout the woods.

The rest of the men ran out of the graveyard before making any further observations. They tripped over one another as they squeezed through the gate. The boss in the yellow hard hat jumped clear over the top. He climbed into the bed of the work truck just as the tires spun and it zoomed away.

I ran to the gates of the cemetery, closing my hands around the bars. "Is it a ghost, Cody Belle? Do you see anything?"

"That's not a ghost." Mr. Marcum laughed. "That's Peri."

"When did he get a bicycle?" Mrs. Marcum asked.

It wasn't just any bicycle Uncle Periwinkle rode out of the woods that day. The bike was spray-painted gold. With his long beard billowing in the wind, and the basket on the front overflowing with flowers, Peri laughed happily as he sped toward us down the brick path. The horn attached to the handlebars made another terrible squeaky-scream sound. "Emma! Come quick! There's something you gotta see down on Starbloom Farm!"

"What . . . wait! Slow down, Uncle Peri!" I shouted as I tossed my sign aside.

"Open the gate!" Peri hollered. "I forgot how to stop!"

"I don't have the key!" I yelled just as Uncle Peri crashed his bike into the other side of the gate. By the time we'd all rushed forward to see if he was okay, Peri was already standing up, laughing. He brushed the dirt from his jeans. "Greta says I can't tell you what's happening on the farm, because you'll never believe it. We have to show you. Come quick. You can bring Cody Belle."

"Can Earl come?" I asked. Then I looked back. "You don't have to if you don't want to."

But Earl nodded like he was game.

"Of course!" Peri said. "Bring Earl! The more the merrier!"

The front door of the Boneyard slapped shut, and my brother jogged down the steps. He came to stand beside us, fists propped on his hips, and looked all around.

"Lose something?" I asked.

Topher shook his head. "I just thought I saw . . . somebody . . ." He shivered. He pressed his hand to the back of his neck. "Never mind."

He walked back inside with a sad look in his eyes.

Just as the door closed behind him, I saw Waverly Valentine push her bicycle away from behind the old shed. She wore a pink camellia stuck in her ponytail. Before she mounted her bike, she reached for the back of her neck, the same as Topher had. She looked toward us and waved.

She pedaled away so quietly, so fast, as if she had experience at disappearing. As if she had the ability to come and go as she pleased without leaving any tracks behind.

Quiet as a whisper.

Lonely as a ghost.

CHAPTER TWELVE

"Get ready, Earl Chance!" I yelled over my shoulder as I pumped my bike pedals.

Cody Belle and Earl followed close behind as we biked to the top of a high green hill. I'd let Earl ride my new bicycle, and I'd fished my old one out of the shed. Being perpetually small has some perks, and this was one of them: My old bicycle wasn't too uncomfortable. I'd kind of missed the feeling of the streamers on the handles flappity-flapping against my hands.

It occurred to me that the last time I'd been on this bike, my mom had been close by. She wasn't a memory back then. She was real and in-person and beside me. For a heartbeat second, I wished my old bike was a time machine that would take me back to her, just long enough to hug her again.

I kicked out my leg at the top of the hill and came to a stop. Cody Belle's bike screeched to a stop on my right side. Earl paused at my left. I watched the reaction on his face as he stared into the valley below. His lips parted, and I wondered if he might speak. He didn't. But his mouth formed a single word: *Wow.*

Starbloom Farm is nestled down in a valley, surrounded by sloped green hills. A white barn anchors the property in the middle, only a short walk from the old farmhouse Aunt Greta and Uncle Peri call home. But the house and the barn aren't the first thing most people notice, Earl Chance included.

First, you see flowers.

Thousands of flowers circle the house and barn, blooming up into the hills. From an angel's point of view, I believe, Starbloom Farm looks like a big quilt, patched together by blooming, firework colors. As we watched, the wind whispered across those blooms, carrying the smell of lavender and a warm summer day.

"I'll lead the way," I said. "Careful on this hill, Earl."

"Emma and I have wiped out here more than a few times," Cody Belle explained.

I agreed with my BFF. "Wiping out is a common side effect of our adventuring. But it's the most fun when you go fast."

I perched my bike at the top of the hill and kicked off, down the dirt path to the barn. As I zoomed past the flowers, the colors blurred together, like a dream. I felt the roller-coaster zoom deep in my belly. Warm wind prickled against my face.

"Onward!" Cody Belle shouted as she charged down the hill behind me. Earl never shouted, but I hoped he was filled with the quiet joy that existed in that place.

The three of us tossed our bikes in the grass near the welcome sign:

GRETA'S MAGICAL GARDEN:

GET YOUR FLOWERS—THEN GO AWAY

"Peri's already here," Cody Belle said, pointing to the golden bicycle propped against the barn. "He might have forgotten how to stop, but he's a speedy rider!"

"I'm glad he's here." I planted my feet and slid open the heavy barn doors. "We need to see whatever amazing discovery this is, then get back to treasure hunting."

Earl's eyes filled with wonder as he stepped inside, spinning in a slow circle to take it all in.

While the barn looks all proper-barn-like from the outside, the inside is quite different. Aunt Greta remodeled the place to serve as her flower shop, so the barn is bursting with blooms. Dozens of flowers are growing up tall trellises, wrapped around old furniture, and creeping up the walls. The three long tables stretched across the barn floor are always covered in flowers ready to be bundled for customers.

Aunt Greta taped notes above the bundles she'd been assembling:

A bouquet of sympathy to Alice McKee,
on the loss of her grandmother

A bouquet of congratulations to Evona Marcum,
for winning Most Robust & Rollicking Tomato Plant
of the Season

"Aunt Greta?" I called out.

"Back here, darlin'!" Aunt Greta yelled. We raced toward the pergola in the corner of the barn, where Greta sat with a clipboard in her arms. Tiny blue Mason jars were hanging from the pergola slats, each one holding different-colored bursts of daisies. Greta was scribbling notes about the flowers, mumbling to herself and probably talking to the blooms occasionally. She likes to pretend she's an old grouch, but I've seen her speak sweetly to the flowers on many occasions.

"Uncle Peri said you had something to show me," I said as I bounced over beside her scooter. "I don't mean to sound pushy but we're in a bit of a hurry and . . ."

"Oh, *pffft*. You've got time for this, Emma!" Greta said as she steered her scooter out of the daisy area. Greta pulled the walkie-talkie from the front basket.

"Periwinkle!" she said into the crackly speaker. "The kids are here."

"Yep," crackled Periwinkle's voice. "On my way. Go ahead and show her the magic flowers first."

"Magic flowers?" Cody Belle squealed.

Greta nodded. "It's my favorite magic, darlin'. The best magic. Science!"

So help me, Aunt Greta actually smirked.

Cody Belle stilled. She yanked me close and whispered, "Is your aunt Greta actually smiling?"

"I think so," I said, surprised by the sight of it. "And I think she giggled. Something strange is in the air for sure."

Most people on a scooter would have paused and gently navigated the sloping hill behind the barn. But Aunt Greta is not most people. She careened down the hill so fast, dirt spun in her wake. We ran behind her—a little breathless trying to keep up—all the way into the woods. Aunt Greta led us to a thicket of tall spruce trees, all so thick your fingertips wouldn't touch if you tried to hug them. Dense vines roped around each tree trunk.

"Now," Greta said, and pointed. "You see all these white, bell-shaped flowers blooming from the vines on these trees?"

"Yes, ma'am." I reached for one of the pale blooms. "They look like lilies."

"Ah, but they're not." Greta clapped her hand on her knee. "Kids, there are three kinds of flowers that only bloom here in Blackbird Hollow. I call them the Oddities.

In all my years of study and botanical explorations, I've never seen the Oddities—or heard of them—anywhere but here in the Hollow.

"First, we have Keeping Susans. Girls around here used to put their wedding dress in a box of Keeping Susans," Greta said. "Or tuck the blossoms into a letter, to keep the ink from running in the rain. Pin them with the clothes on the line, to keep the sun from fading the color. Keeping Susans still grow around here, but not as much as they used to."

"Blue keeps them in the pantry," I said, not meaning to sound impatient. But flowers did not tell me things about treasure.

"The second Oddity is called a Starbloom. Every so often, a hiker finds one in the woods, but they're almost extinct now. And that's a shame. Starblooms could heal all kinds of ailments."

"Why don't you find some for your hip?" I asked.

"Oh, that would take more Starblooms than we have left. We can't even find one for here at the farm. The flower is pale blue and star-shaped, and under a full moon it shines as if somebody dipped it in glitter."

Cody Belle elbowed me hard.

"I've seen one," I said suddenly.

"Then you're as rare as they are!" Greta beamed. "They've all but died out now. I've heard when the moon shimmers over those petals, they look like stars on earth.

"And then there's a third Oddity. And that's the kind of flower that I wanted to show you. These are the Telling Vines. And they do something extraordinary . . ."

Extraordinary.

Like my ancestors.

Like me, maybe. Hopefully. If I ever found that blasted treasure. "Aunt Greta, we really have to . . ."

Suddenly, Uncle Peri ran out the back door of the barn, his beard billowing in the breeze behind him. "It's coming!" he yelled. "The wind's coming. Get ready, kids! The Gypsy Roses are 'bout to blow!"

As if we'd summoned them out of the air, a warm wind whooshed through the forest . . . bringing with it the red rain of the Gypsy Roses.

"Okay, now!" Aunt Greta yelled over the wind. "Get close to those flowers, kids! Cup them gently against your ear. And listen . . ."

We each ran to a different tree. And waited.

At first, the woods were full of wind . . . but then, voices.

Hundreds of voices.

And the voices . . . they came from the Telling Vines.

I cupped a flower against my ear and listened, the same way I'd listened to a seashell once, trying to hear the ocean.

Faintly, a young woman's voice came from inside.

I'll never forget you, Ernest Lee. I moved on, like you asked me to. But my heart stayed there with you.

"Hot dog!" Cody Belle grinned as she reached above me and pulled the flower down so we could both hear it. The bloom held the gentle voice of an old man:

This here is a message for my son. And I want him to know that I'm sorry for what I did, and I love him more than anything.

Earl tapped my pant leg. He was kneeling beside the tree, listening to one of the low-growing vines. The flower held a woman's voice, caught on a sob:

I love you, Begonia McIntyre. You are my heart.

"Emma!" Cody Belle yelled. She held a vine dangling from an old branch. "This one's got the jamboree song in it! 'Darlin' Daisy'!"

The song, sung in a small child's voice, repeated over and over in the bloom.

Darlin' Daisy, lace your boots up,
Take the lantern, shine it bright . . .

"And that's what I call magic!" Aunt Greta grinned. "As I said, these flowers only bloom here in Blackbird Hollow. The message you leave in a Telling Vine can only be heard by the intended recipient. Unless the Gypsy Roses are blowing."

"They all have messages inside them?" I asked.

"Many do." Peri smiled as he pulled down another

Telling Vine for me to hear. "People used to send love letters in the Telling Vines. A lady might whisper *I love you* into a flower and tuck it in her beloved's pocket when he marched off to war. Sometimes, before a person drew their last breath, they'd ask for a Telling Vine. Leave a message for someone who didn't get a chance to say good-bye."

"How did they all end up here?" I asked. "I mean, once you pluck a flower . . . it's dead, right?"

Uncle Peri shook his head and grinned. "That's a funny thing about Telling Vines. During a Gypsy Rose summer, the vines are full of old messages."

Peri walked past a vine and touched one of the blooms. A young girl's voice called out, as mighty as the wind:

Be brave, sweet Cillian. Come home to me.

"Greta and I have made a special project of finding as many as we can, and moving them here. To preserve them, you see. Especially now that Warren Steele's digging up the entire mountain. There are so few left as it is."

Greta nodded proudly. "Warren's determined to snuff out the history of these hills. He might scar the mountain's face with his bulldozer. He might send a wrecking ball through every last barn in the county. But the stories?" She shook her head fiercely. "He can't touch those. Stories are made to last. It's our job, I believe, to make sure the stories keep blooming."

"These are outstanding," I sighed.

Aunt Greta waved Earl and Cody Belle closer to listen to a particularly funny flower. Uncle Peri leaned down and whispered to me, "There's one in particular I thought you might want to hear, little Emma." He winked at me. "Just don't tell Granny Blue."

I touched the bloom he pointed to, and listened. The voice belonged to a little girl. Her message was a brave and urgent whisper:

Find Lily Kate. She knows the way.

The Conductor holds the key.

CHAPTER THIRTEEN

"The Conductor holds the key," I whispered as we pulled our bikes from Uncle Peri's truck. Due to the impending storm, he'd given us a lift back to the cafe. Peri whistled his way toward some Boneyard Brew. My fellow explorers and I meandered more slowly inside, so we could treasure talk.

"Lily Kate definitely knew the Conductor," I said. "That has to be what the clue in the vine means."

Cody Belle shivered and pulled her arm through mine. "It's a good thing we didn't dig up the grave."

I turned to Earl, who had an appropriately creeped-out look on his face. "We're not crazies who dig up graves," I assured him. "I just thought that particular grave might be a front for hiding treasure. It could still be that, I guess. The treasure might be buried with Lily Kate. But if that's the case, she can definitely keep it."

"You heard the Conductor's song, Emma," Cody Belle said. "I think the ghost wants you to find the treasure. And since this ghost was—obviously—friends with Lily Kate, he wouldn't want you being a creepy grave digger in order to do that. I think the grave is a clue."

I looked at Earl and wished he'd say something. Earl has an honest look about him, the kind of face that makes me think he would have sincere and valuable insight. Just having him around on our adventures made me feel more at ease, even though he didn't contribute in words. I already had a feeling Earl was a rare friend, the kind of person who makes a place seem more pleasant, more calm, just because he's there.

Granny Blue pushed the door open and waved us inside. "Y'all look like you're up to no good out here. Come in and drink some hot cocoa."

We thundered up the steps and into the cafe. Blue patted Earl's shoulder. "Good to see you again, Mr. Chance! Why don't you pop back in the kitchen with me for a second? See if an apple fritter strikes your fancy? We love newcomers here in the Hollow. Fritters are on us this week."

Earl's a wise young man, because he followed Blue back to the kitchen with a smile on his face and a bounce in his step.

Cody Belle and I snagged our corner table.

"While Earl's on Fritter Duty, let's recap our clues," I said as I stuck a daisy in my hair.

Cody Belle opened our page of treasure notes.

<u>Stuff We Know about the Loot</u>
The Conductor led Emma to Lily Kate's grave.
Find Lily Kate. She knows the way.
The Conductor holds the key.

"And, of course, the symbol on the grave." Cody Belle turned the page to the star that'd been carved on Lily Kate's gravestone.

I traced the image with my fingertip. "I know there's a treasure, Cody Belle. We're so close. I can feel it. We just need to figure out where to dig."

I scanned the notes again, tapping a pen against the table in a quick snappity-pop rhythm. Sometimes my mind works faster when I listen to music. "Okay," I said as an idea took shape. "Lily Kate lived around the time of the Civil War. Everybody believes the Conductor was a Civil War soldier. Blackbird Hollow has a weird Civil War history. So maybe we need some more clues about the time period. Uncle Peri!" I hollered. He popped out from the kitchen holding a chocolate-covered spoon. I waved him closer.

"I want to talk about the Conductor's treasure on

graveyard tours. Do you know anything else about him? Or anything about the Civil War in Blackbird Hollow?"

"The Conductor is a mystery." He clapped his hands and settled in close to us. "But I can tell you some interesting facts. Unlike most of the state of Tennessee, lots of the mountain people, like Blackbird Hollow, did not side with the Confederacy. They had no desire to secede from the United States. Tennessee was the last state to secede from the Union, but Blackbird Hollow tried to hang in there. For forty-eight hours, Blackbird Hollow became the Independent State of Blackbird Hollow. Many men left to fight for the Union cause. That's true of every war, though. That's why Tennessee is called the Volunteer State, you know. In every war, more men volunteered to go."

"Men *and* women," I said.

"Yes!" Peri agreed.

"Sometimes they'd follow their beloveds into war," I said to Cody Belle. "Other times, they'd dress like men so they could fight. And some people fought without ever pulling a trigger." I pulled the Book of Days from my bag and pointed out an entry to Cody Belle.

Rachel Miller

The Renegade

I, Rachel Miller, had the blue flower dream of my ancestors when I was fourteen years old.

My dream was more of a nightmare, though. In the field of blue flowers, I saw my family huddled together. Mama was sobbing. Daddy's face was twisted in fear. "I'll protect you," I said to them, surprised by the strength of my small voice.

I woke up covered in sweat. For the first time I could remember, I was more fearful than excited about my destiny. I'd only ever been Rachel—sweet and shy, a girl who loved books and animals and red roses. I wasn't bold like the rest of my family. My father'd made our barn a hiding place for deserters—soldiers who'd defected from both sides of the war, who only wanted to get home to the people they loved. But I feared that once my dream came true, the hiding place on our farm wouldn't be enough . . . for them or for us.

Nothing could prepare me for the fear that took hold of me on the day Confederate soldiers came looking for my father. I was in town when I first saw them. I heard them ask where my father lived.

"Hide in the woods," I yelled as I ran inside my house.

I leaned down and looked into my little brother's teary eyes. "You remember the hiding places?"

He nodded, resolute.

My dad stood his ground, though his chin trembled as he looked at me. He wanted to stay.

"They'll take you if they find you," I said, grabbing his arm. "Go hide in the woods."

My family—and the soldiers we hid—had barely run past the tree line when I heard the sound of horses' hooves hammering down the path. I'd never felt smaller than I did that day, walking out into the yard to meet them. My heart raced.

The soldier in front asked to see my father.

"He's not here," I answered.

The soldier cocked his head at me. "Then where is he?"

He vowed to burn down our home if I refused to tell him. But I clenched my fists and said nothing. I watched through tears as our house and barn disappeared in flames. Ashes floated through the air like sinister snowflakes, settling on the wilted rose garden. But I would not tell the location of my family. The soldier finally motioned for his men to go . . . but not before he turned, raised his arm, and hit me across the face with the butt of his rifle.

The scar he left was permanent, and so was the blindness in that eye. Some folks thought of me as a hero. I was asked to speak at rallies, churches, and schoolhouses, mostly *because people wanted to see the little girl who fought the big army. They wanted bloody details.*

But I talked about forgiveness and family. I talked about learning to rebuild a farm and a life, even though we started from ashes. I couldn't stop trembling the first time I spoke. But I always walked out with my head held high and my family close to me.

My admonition to future generations is this: Sometimes even doing the right thing will leave you with scars. But beauty comes from ashes, too. And I know that to be true.

"She kept people in the Hollow safe when the soldiers came," I told Cody.

Peri nodded. "There's all kinds of caves and woods here—hiding places. I've heard soldiers who ran away from the war hid out there."

Hiding places. There were hundreds of hiding places here. How would I ever find the one place that hid my treasure?

The door screech-banged shut again and Waverly Valentine stepped into the room. Her dress was silver gray and short, with little pink flowers all over it. It was the kind of dress that's perfect for dancing, the kind of dress that ripples like water when you spin around. She wore her funky glasses, too.

"Waverly!" I pushed out the extra chair at our table. "Sit with us!"

"I saw the sign outside," Waverly said quietly as she settled into the chair.

Granny Blue walked past the table and refilled our Boneyard Brew. "The sign that says 'Beware of Goat'?"

Waverly shook her head. She grinned sheepishly. "The sign that says you have fresh-made lavender-peach muffins?"

"You are a muffin aficionado, Waverly Valentine." I meant it as a compliment. I have so much respect for people who know how to appreciate quality baked goods. Blue pushed a basket in front of Waverly.

"We'll have another fresh batch out of the oven in no time," Blue assured her. "Emma, your buddy Earl's back there sampling a new recipe for me. He'll be out shortly."

"Whoa." Waverly shivered. She dropped her muffin and pressed a trembling hand to the back of her neck. Before I could explain the Touch, she said, "I have an important question. The shortest route back to the trail is through the Wailing Woods. Since this whole town is haunted, I'm guessing there's a ghost or two in there, right? How much will that part of the journey freak me out?"

"I've never seen a ghost there," Cody Belle said. "But I don't like the Wailing Woods. Sadness presses down on me in those woods."

"Unfortunately, that makes perfect sense," Periwinkle

said. "Because ghosts aren't the only things that haunt a place. And the Wailing Woods are proof of that. It's another sad result of the Civil War. There was a battle fought in those woods, and many men died there. For the duration of the battle, the woods were filled with screams and cries. But after that, that's when people heard wailing. They say it's the sound the widows made, mourning their loved ones. Whether or not that's true, I think Miss Chitwood is correct. I think your heart knows sometimes when you step in a place where something tragic's happened. Sorrow has a residue about it, see. Sorrow seeps into the ground. Hovers over a place."

"So the ghosts aren't . . . necessarily . . . bad?" Cody Belle asked.

"I believe there's something watching over us. Call it ghosts, if you want. Or maybe it's our loved ones just peeking in every so often. Maybe nudging us toward our destiny."

"I do believe in destiny," Waverly said. And then she cocked her head as she glanced down at Cody Belle's notebook, still open to the page with the star. "I saw that when I came through the woods. You know where the trail drops off into the forest? I found an old chimney there. And I saw that mark carved into it."

"Ah!" Peri said as he leaned closer and studied the picture. "The only ruins in the Wailing Woods are from Jasper Abernathy's homestead."

I glanced quickly at Cody Belle. She stared back at me, glittery-eyed with excitement. Joy had already replaced her fear. It's addictive, the feeling of adventure. And without words or even actions, I knew we were saying exactly the same thing in our minds:

The Conductor's treasure isn't in the cemetery . . . it's in the woods.

Topher swirled out of the kitchen, carrying a basket. "Who ordered more muffins?" he asked.

The next thing I heard was the sound of Waverly's coffee mug shattering against the floor.

Topher stilled. His eyes were wide and his face was set. You'd think somebody waved a magic wand and turned my brother into a love-struck statue.

"You," Waverly said through clenched teeth. An angry zigzag of pink hair fell down over her forehead. Like a lightning bolt.

I saw my brother's throat ripple with a nervous swallow. "Waverly?" he said softly. "How are you . . . here?"

She didn't reply. She just stared deep into my brother's eyes. And I'm here to tell you, whatever invisible thing connected those two was thick enough to feel, even if you weren't directly in their line of fire. Waverly rose slowly from the table. I wondered if she might run at my brother, like a scene in a movie. Maybe throw her arms around his neck and kiss him, and effectively make it one of the most awkward days of my short life. But that is not what she did.

"Waverly?" Topher said again, taking a step toward her.

Waverly's lips pressed into a firm line. She picked up the muffin from the table and flung it at my brother with the calculated fury of a top-notch softball pitcher. Topher ducked as the muffin sailed over his head and bounced off the wall. He overturned the basket of muffins in the process; they tumbled with a plop-plop-plop across the floor.

I saw a tear roll down Waverly's face before she spun around in a swirl of silver and ran out the cafe door.

"Love always seems to come from the places we least expect." Granny Blue patted Topher's shoulder. "It would appear love came to Waverly from the general direction of the kitchen."

"How do you know Waverly?" I asked Topher.

He began to answer, but couldn't find the words. He started toward the kitchen and turned around again. Finally, he set his face in determination and ran out the front door after her.

Periwinkle chuckled and unfolded his newspaper again. "There's something that draws people here. If you end up in Blackbird Hollow, there's a reason. You might ought to find out what it is."

"I think we should definitely follow them and eavesdrop," Cody Belle said.

"Concentrate, Cody Belle!" I said as I gave her shoulders a shake. "We've got to go find the treasure first. Then we'll fix my brother's love life. Go get Earl and meet me outside."

"Where are you going?"

"To the shed. I need to assemble a treasure-hunting kit!"

When I ran out on the front porch, the skies were growing darker over the Wailing Woods. I'd always known those woods held secrets.

I was about to find the best secret of all.

CHAPTER FOURTEEN

The sky above the Wailing Woods rolled smoky gray. Our shoes squished in the mud. Bright green leaves rustled overhead, tossing a rain-echo back and forth among the trees. The rain had cooled things off considerably in town, but the woods are always cooler, rain or not.

Cody Belle had snorkel-goggles pushed over her eyes and she carried a compass in her hand.

"What are these for again?" she asked, tapping the goggles.

I shrugged. "I saw them in the shed and thought we might need them. It never hurts to be prepared. As for this"—I lifted the metal detector I carried over my shoulder like a fishing pole—"I thought it might expedite the process. Uncle Peri used to rent it to tourists looking for Civil War relics."

Between Cody Belle and me, I wasn't sure if we looked more like bona fide explorers or the grand marshals of the dork parade. I'd taken charge of the map for a bit, mostly just to look official. I've never been good at reading them, though. Maps look like tangled Christmas lights to me. Earl Chance, on the other hand, was a natural. He'd been back in town less than a week, but seemed to orient himself quick and easy. He'd lean down to study our location, then pull his goggles back over his eyes and lead the way.

The kid was a natural explorer.

Cody Belle stopped and propped her hand on her hip. "Which way now, Marco Polo?"

Earl consulted the map and pointed straight ahead, through a thicket of tall maple trees.

"Map readers are magical people," said Cody Belle. She let Earl get a few strides ahead of us before she lowered her voice and asked, "Do you think he'll ever talk again?"

"I don't know. I hope so."

CAW CAW!

"Penny Lane!" I spun around and looked up toward the shadowy bird swooping through the treetops. "I love the sound of her squawking."

"You love the sound a crow makes?" Cody Belle asked.

"I do if the crow's Penny Lane. These are my most favorite sounds, though: old hymns carried on fragile voices, rain on the roof, Bear's paws tap-tap-tapping across the floor, shooting stars—"

"Those don't make a sound," Cody Belle said.

"That's what I like about them. I like thinking that something as mighty as a star can move across the universe that way. Without a sound or a scream or anything. It just dances. Just burns a quiet path across the night."

CAW CAW!

"Penny Lane agrees," I said. "That's the farthest she's been from home in ever!"

"I can't believe Penny Lane's still following you around," Cody Belle said. "That crow's as faithful as an old dog. I—*WHOA!*"

Cody Belle slipped on the edge of a ravine. I lunged for her, and grabbed her arm. But the mud was too slippery . . . so I slid down next. Earl Chance grabbed on to me, but we all lost our balance and slid down the hillside. We landed with a

WHOP

WHOP

WHOP

in the muddy hollow down below.

"Ugh." Cody Belle's hands made a suction sound as she pulled them loose from the thick mud. "Thank goodness for these." She peeled her muddy goggles away from her face and perched them in her hair. "Penny Lane, you were a distraction!"

"Maybe Penny Lane knows we're going the wrong way," I said as I pulled my hands free of the sticky mud.

Earl reached out and touched my arm. When I looked at him, a big smile broke across his face. For a heartbeat-second, I couldn't look away. Something about Earl's smile connected directly with my heart. His smile was so big and genuine. So . . . happy.

He pointed straight ahead. And then he looked directly at me and caught me looking directly at him. My face felt warm, like the start of a sunburn, but there was no sun right then. Just Earl.

"That's it!" Cody Belle screeched.

Nestled in the woods up ahead of us was a tall, old stone chimney. It looked exactly the way Waverly had described it, too. There was no house attached to the chimney any-more—not a floorboard, a door, or even a brick to be seen. Moss grew thick around the chimney's base, and creeping ivy wrapped all the way to the tallest rock on the chimney. It was made of long, flat stones piled wide to make a small fireplace, then narrowing toward the tip-top. Penny Lane perched proudly on the chimney's corner.

Earl stood and reached to help me and Cody up off the ground. We were stuck so deep in the mud that he nearly fell over again as he pulled us upright.

I realized ivy wasn't the only plant covering the chim-ney. All three of us saw the Telling Vine at the same time.

"Hold it where we can all hear it," I said to Cody Belle, my voice full of awestruck wonder. Cody Belle tugged gently at the vine, pulling one of the white-bell flowers around. We all leaned in so close to hear it that my forehead was nearly touching Earl's.

Seeing the flower in Cody Belle's hand reminded me of catching fireflies in our hands when we were kids. I remembered how we cupped our hands and whispered wishes before we let the fireflies go. And then we watched those wishes float away into the woods, burning bright little holes into the darkness. We'd always known, deep down, that something about the Hollow was special, full of things that bloom and glow and fly. The Telling Vine was a true, blooming miracle.

A gentle wind blew, and we all heard the message inside immediately. But this message was nothing new. All we heard was "Darlin' Daisy," sung in the slow, soft voice of a little girl:

"Catch a little star,
Put it in your pocket,
But don't forget to wait for me."

"That's not much help." Cody Belle reached out to touch the stone underneath with her muddy fingertips.

"Somebody probably sang it when they lived here. This seems like a sad place, doesn't it?" I said. "No, not sad. Sacred. I mean, this used to be a house. A whole family lived here. Years ago, people sat beside this fireplace and told stories and ate dinner. It's like a gravestone, sort of. It marks a whole lifetime's worth of memories."

Cody Belle released the Telling Vine. The words of the old folk song floated around us, a lonely echo.

Earl stepped around me and crouched down in front of the fireplace. He reached toward a flat, long stone. There in the corner, underneath his fingertip, was the same star we'd found on Lily Kate Abernathy's grave.

With a shaking hand, I reached out to trace it. " 'Beneath the stars of Blackbird Hollow.' " I swallowed. " 'By the shadows of the ridge . . .' "

"We're near the ridge," Cody Belle said, leaning down beside me. "We're surrounded by tree shadows. But . . . 'down a path no man can follow'?"

"No man but Earl Chance." I elbowed him playfully.

"Maybe Lily Kate Abernathy hid the treasure under her house and marked it with this star," Cody Belle said. "And somebody who loved her deeply put the mark on her grave after she was gone, as a tribute. It could be right here . . ."

"It's possible," I whispered.

Everything wonderful is possible. My mom used to say that. The memory of her voice blew across my heart like a soft breeze. And it was gone just as quickly.

Earl reached for the metal detector and raised his eyebrow.

"Does it still work?" I asked. "Or did we crush it when we fell?"

Cody Belle turned on the metal detector, which made a faint buzzing sound as it whirred to life. Earl and I followed as she walked slowly around the chimney.

"It looks like you're vacuuming dirt," I told her.

"*Shh*," she said. And suddenly, the detector made a *ZRRP ZRRP ZRRP* noise.

"Right here!" she yelled. "Dig right here!"

"Today's the day we find untold riches!" I said as I fished through my bag and handed Earl and Cody Belle tiny gardening trowels. "We'll save the cafe!"

I could picture my name there, in the Book of Days. I could write my entry as soon as I got home.

Emma Pearl Casey
The Adventurer!

I found the key that unlocked the great treasure of Blackbird Hollow! I saved my family's home! I brought wealth and riches back to my town! My life changed here!

I would be connected to my mom. Forever. Tonight.

Cody Belle squinted her eyes at the trowels. "This is what we're digging with?"

"It's all I could find in the shed," I said, squatting down on the ground.

"Hope this chimney doesn't fall on us while we work," Cody Belle said as we began scraping. And I do mean scraping; my trowels wouldn't unearth more than a handful of dirt at a time.

"Hope there aren't any snakes," Cody Belle mumbled.

Clink.

"I found something!" Cody Belle's eyes were as wild as a mad scientist's.

"Push the dirt away carefully," I told her, tossing my trowel to the side. "The treasure might be fragile! We don't want it to shatter!"

"I see it!" Cody Belle said, leaning down low.

"Me, too." My heart thumped so loud I couldn't hear what I was saying.

We unearthed a rusted metal box partially covered in rocks. The box was so small that I lifted it easily out of the ground, and pulled it into my lap.

"This is so light," I said nervously. "It should be heavy, right? A treasure this important should be heavy?"

Cody Belle scooted close beside me. "Just open it, Emma."

I pried it open with the trowel.

There was no gold inside.

"It's just flowers?" Cody Belle asked.

"Keeping Susans," I said, scooping out a handful of blooms. The weight of flower petals in my hand was heart-breaking at first. Because I'd hoped for something heavier: gold or riches—or my key, at least. The flowers were special, of course. But they wouldn't save my home. They looked so flimsy, like pale yellow wings in my palm. I closed my eyes and tried to wish away the disappointment pressing down on me.

Cody Belle nudged against me. "Hey, if they're Keeping Susans, that means they're keeping something preserved, right?"

"Probably not a treasure, though," I said, sifting through the flowers in the metal box as if they were packing peanuts. I still hoped my fingers would brush against the cold metal of a key . . .

But all I found was an old hymnal. The cover was pale green, faded a bit despite the work of the Keeping Susans. It was softer than I thought it would be. Something about it reminded me of an old blanket, or an old teddy bear. When you love a thing, it looks worn out in a good way, a better way, the more you hold it. *Life Songs*, the title read in letters that were probably a brighter gold many years ago.

The book crackled when I opened it; the sound reminded me of my book. The Book of Days.

"Oh!" I said, leaning down to read the inscription inside. Someone had written the name of the cafe . . . before it was the cafe.

Blackbird Hollow Community Church, 1850
For where your treasure is, there will your heart be also.
(Matthew 6:21)

"It's beautiful," I said.

"But it's not a treasure," Cody Belle said, leaning into me. "I'm sorry, Emma." To my great surprise, Earl Chance leaned closer to me, too. They both looked at me the way you do when you really care about someone, when you wish you could split a person's sorrows like a stale candy bar and share them.

Somebody'd cared enough about that hymnal to surround it with Keeping Susans and bury it like a time capsule. So I saved it. I tucked it into my bag beside the Book of Days.

The hymnal was a lovely find, but it wasn't the treasure that would save the cafe.

I looked up at the patches of sky visible above the woods and felt like everything was slipping away.

"We'll find it, Emma," Cody Belle said quietly. Earl squeezed my arm. He barely knew me and he believed in me, too.

"Yes," I said, quietly but with revved-up hope in my heart. "We will find it."

Suddenly, the ground began to shake and roar with such force that I wondered if the earth might burp. Or swallow us. Or both.

"Is that an earthquake?" Cody Belle asked, scrambling to her feet to look around.

I launched off the ground and grabbed her and Earl and pulled them away from the old chimney. "If it is, we shouldn't be near the chimney. It could crush us to bits."

"The trees will crush us before the chimney will," she yelled.

But the roar from the ground turned into the more distinct growl of a motor. Lots of motors.

"Ugh," Cody Belle groaned. "I know what that sound is. It's worse than a natural disaster."

She held the metal detector in front of her like a sword.

We watched as four four-wheelers raced up to the edge of the ravine, one by one.

A fifth four-wheeler, bright pink with glitter-flames on the sides, spun up in the middle of the group. The driver revved her engine once, then pulled off her helmet.

Beretta Simpson.

I had a sudden urge to crawl in the old chimney and hide.

"Don't let her smell your fear," Cody Belle whispered, pivoting to stand in front of me. Beretta cleared her throat and studied us one by one. "It's the ghost girl and her faithful sidekick, Trailer Trash. And you." She fluttered her eyelashes at Earl. "I remember you. Why are you with them?"

"Why are you here?" Cody Belle asked. "Now that you've said hi, you can carry on. We're busy."

Cody Belle was no fun to mess with, and Beretta knew this. Beretta pressed her mouth into a flat line and stared at my face. My fingers twitched painfully; I wanted to cover my scar. I wanted to pull my T-shirt up over my nose, turtle-tuck half my face so she couldn't see me.

Cody Belle leaned into me, barely whispering. "Do not cover your mouth."

But that's what Beretta stared at: my mouth. My scar. She looked me in the eye and said nothing, but her unspoken promise was loud and clear: The next school year would be no better than this past one. I couldn't think of any other person who enjoyed being cruel the way she did. It would be one thing if I was a jerk to her, if I regularly dished out insults in an effort to make her days as crummy as she made mine. But I hadn't. In all the years I'd known her, I'd never tried to get in her way. I had actively tried to stay away from her.

Beretta looked at Earl next. "You can do way better. She's not even pretty."

Earl ducked his head, and at first I thought he was embarrassed. Embarrassed to be seen with me. Embarrassed to be wearing goggles and carrying a metal detector and looking for stupid buried treasure like we were little kids.

He didn't speak. But he stepped up beside me, until his arm was touching mine. And he stared at Beretta Simpson as if she didn't scare him at all.

As if her words didn't matter.

"Oh . . . I forgot you weren't talking now," Beretta said, scrunching her face in mock sympathy. She looked at her minions. "One little boom of thunder and Earl peed his pants and forgot how to talk." Her friends all giggled.

"Grow up, Beretta," I snapped.

"Calm down, smiley," Beretta said, cocking her head at me. "See you in sixth grade." And she spun her tires to toss mud down into the ravine and drove away.

Cody wiped the mud off her face. "As far as wild-animal encounters go, that one wasn't so bad."

"I need some Boneyard Brew," I sighed. "Back to the cafe to figure out what to do next?"

"I have to go home first," Cody Belle said. "But I'll meet you there later. Don't give up, Emma. We'll find it."

But I had my doubts.

We walked Cody Belle back to Sweet Peaches. Before she split, I reminded her it was a jamboree night. I didn't want to miss a dance at the cafe, especially since we probably didn't have many left.

"Don't give up, Emma," she said again as she gave me a squeezingly tight hug. "We still have time."

But we didn't have time. Not at all. Warren Steele had already sent his men to survey the land, and Blue had the papers set to sign. It was just a matter of days. Maybe less.

Earl walked home beside me. I thought he might split, too, when we got close enough to the path near his house. But he didn't, and we walked on in silence for a while. Maybe the fact that he couldn't talk was what caused me to open up.

And I mean open up, like spill out a waterfall of thoughts.

"I have a theory about Beretta Simpson," I said to Earl. "She has a rare and unusual gift. Whatever you're most sensitive or insecure about, she knows it. It's like she can see the invisible target on a person's heart and ZAP—she goes right for it."

We emerged from the woods and walked into the cemetery. The setting sun was peeking out through the shattered sky, casting pink and gold light across the stormy underbelly. The cafe looked beautiful in the fading light. Maybe knowing my days there were limited made it look even more beautiful than usual. Sometimes you don't realize how special a place—or a person—really is until they're slipping away from you.

"I guess she's the least of my worries, though. For right now, anyway. This place is my sanctuary. My mom loved it here. My dad, too, probably."

I spoke softly. I didn't think Earl had heard me. But then he unzipped my bag and pulled out a notebook. He scribbled a note for me to read.

I know your mom is gone. What happened to your dad?

"He died before I was born," I said, handing the notebook back. "I don't talk about it, because I think people feel sorry for me enough as it is."

He turned the page and scribbled a new note.

Does living beside a graveyard bother you?

"No." I plucked a dandelion from the grass and stuck it in my braid. "I know this sounds weird, but I think about death so much anyway . . . that it almost makes me feel better to be here. To try and find out stories about the dearly departed. They're not just names to me. Know what I mean?"

Before I could ask Earl if he wanted the full tour experience, he scribbled something else in the book.

My sanctuary is under my house. I feel safe there.

"You aren't afraid of rats?" I asked.

He grinned, and shook his head no.

"That makes sense. A guy who explores this cemetery at night isn't afraid of anything . . . Are you ever going to tell me what you were looking for out here that night?"

He looked at me as though he wanted to tell me. But he said nothing. Instead, Earl sat down pretzel-style beside a grave and turned the page. I tossed my bag on the ground and sat down beside him while he scribbled.

Earl passed me the notebook.

What's your deal with Beretta Simpson? What'd she do to you?

I didn't answer at first. I let the wind fill the silence between us. A few rose petals tangled in the grass, and I picked one up. Pressed it between my fingers. Earl scooted closer, until his knees were touching my knees. And he waited.

"It's more what she said than what she did," I finally told him. "I have this scar, here—"

I touched the small zigzag scar above my mouth. "When I was born, my mouth looked different. It's called a cleft lip. I had surgery to fix it when I was a baby. But it still looked different in school. You don't remember?"

He shook his head. He watched my mouth as I spoke. My fingers twitched with a desire to cover it. "I had more surgeries as I got older. My last one was two summers ago. My scar's not as obvious now. But when we were little kids, Beretta used to push up one side of her lip and pretend to be me, and her friends laughed at her doing it. And then they'd all smile goofy and lopsided and say, *'Look—I'm Emma!'* because that's how it looked when I smiled, I guess. She still does it. You'd think it wouldn't hurt anymore, but it hurts just as much. And it hurts because I know she'll never stop. She'll always make fun of me."

Earl's eyelashes fluttered. He looked away, toward the tall stones. He looked like he was pondering something important. A hard math problem.

Earl reached for the notebook again and turned to a blank page.

Your smile is what made me want to talk to you. Because it's nice.

He ripped out the page and gave it to me.

My face felt warm and prickly. I nodded. "I like your smile, too," I told him.

He chewed on his lip as he snatched the page back to write something else. Then he passed it to me.

I like your smile because it's different. Cool different. Your smile is pretty.

My face felt sunburnt as I read the page. "Thank you," I said shyly. And I smiled back at him. Really smiled. I didn't try to hide my face or cover my smile. I just grinned. I couldn't stop smiling after that. My cheeks stung from smiling so hard.

"Are you hungry, Earl?" I finally asked him. I folded his note and put it in my bag where I'd remember to pull it out later.

Earl nodded.

I pulled a crumpled bag of BBQ chips from my bag and we shared them, while Gypsy Roses blew over the grounds all around us. I kept talking. Earl kept listening.

These were my favorite sounds right then:

A crinkling bag.

Crunchy chips.

The sheer whisper of wind tangled up in the trees.

Earl's laugh . . . rippling through the air.

I paused, my chip in the air midway to my mouth.

A laugh wasn't talking . . . but it was something. And maybe it was a sign that his voice wasn't far away. Maybe Earl could talk. Maybe . . . he just didn't want to. Not yet.

I tried not to pretend it was a big deal, but I had to admit it: Hanging out with Earl in the graveyard, eating chips, made my heart feel fizzed over. Later on, I'd drum out some thoughts about Earl Chance, and they would be happy like a heartbeat.

CHAPTER FIFTEEN

The dark clouds that had followed us all day long finally gave up a low growl. Earl and I rose to our feet and hurried toward the gate. I told him Topher'd be happy to drive him home, but he shook his head no.

"At least let me walk with you," I said, pushing the gate open for him. But Earl shook his head again, popped his hood, and took off in a long-strided run.

"See you at the jamboree, okay?" I yelled after him. He waved but didn't look back.

I headed back into what would be the cafe for only another few days, if Warren got his way. My heart sank like a bowling ball at the sight of Steele Associates trucks pulled into the grass. The back tire of the red pickup had smashed Blue's favorite iris. Warren's workers were walking around the cafe, making notes, making plans that had nothing to do with me. He'd probably put a wrecking ball through the stained-glass window before the ink dried on Blue's signature.

Blue'd decided to close the restaurant for a few hours that afternoon so Warren's people could have some room to look around. Plus, she needed time to think, she said. Since we had a jamboree that night, I knew the cafe would fill up in short order once we opened back up. At the top of the wooden ramp, a certain spin through the window caught my eye. "The ghost!" I grinned as I raced through the door.

But it wasn't the ghost.

What'd I'd seen was Granny Blue . . . dancing.

She'd turned up the jukebox so loud the walls were vibrating to the sound of recorded steel guitars. As I've said, some songs are fight songs, and they give you the courage to push through an ordeal. But some songs latch on to you, heart-first, and pull you out on the dance floor. Blue was caught up in a dancing song. She was all alone in the cafe, just spinning in circles. She stopped and bowed to an invisible partner, then crooked her arm as if a ghost was holding on tight, ready for *do-si-do*.

I couldn't remember the last time I'd seen her so animated. It nearly made me mad, at first. It was a poor time to dance, considering Warren Steele's deadline pressing down on our shoulders and the Boneyard Cafe in dire straits. But the jamboree nights had also taught me this powerful truth: When life gets heavy, sometimes your heart needs to cut loose. And nobody danced like Blue; she's not elegant or formal about the way she moves. She's not worried about timing. She just lets the music tell her what to do—lets it pull her body this way and that. The way Blue dances is the best kind of dancing; she dances because she's happy, not worried a lick about what people think.

Maybe I should have walked away and let Blue keep dancing by herself. But seeing her so happy filled me with happiness, too. It'd been a long time since I'd seen her grin that way.

She swirled to a stop when she saw me standing in the doorway. "Emma!"

"Sorry to interrupt," I said sheepishly. "I thought you were the kitchen ghost."

She laughed and said, "I figure ghosts are nothing to be afraid of . . . not if you invite them out of the dark places to dance every once in a while."

I walked over to the jukebox and turned the volume down. "You're not just going to give up, are you, Blue? Can't you see how happy this place makes you? You can't just let Warren have it!"

Blue's eyes were suddenly glassy with sadness. Instead of answering my question, she said, "You know what I've been thinking? It's time you learned the secret family recipe for Boneyard Brew."

My heart leaped. "Really?"

Blue nodded.

"But it won't matter soon," I said sadly. "We won't be selling it after that."

"But we'll make it for each other. We'll still pass the recipe—and the secret ingredient—down for generations."

"Like the Book of Days," I said.

Blue sighed. "Something like that. You want to learn to make it or not?"

"Yes!" I ran to the kitchen and tied my too-long apron.

Granny Blue started by pouring thick cream into the Cocoa Cauldron. Then she shaved a block of chocolate and dumped that in the kettle, too.

"Hold the spoon like this," she said. She locked her hands around mine, so I could feel the movements. Then she let me go, and let me try by myself. I wanted to prove to her that I could make Boneyard Brew exactly right. I mean, I don't mind doing dishes at the cafe. We all take turns doing that. But I have way more fun when Topher lets me help him bake. And actually making brew for the Boneyard Cafe? That's bona fide chef stuff.

"Looking good," Blue said approvingly. "Once this last swirl of cream disappears, we'll add the secret ingredient."

"So what *is* the secret ingredient?" I asked her. "Is it the chocolate?"

"Quality chocolate is important." Blue smiled. "But no . . . it's something else."

Blue wiped her hands on her apron and spun around, ducking her head as she stepped into the pantry. She was so tall that she didn't have to tippy-toe to reach the tall shelf.

She returned with a small blue glass jar and unscrewed the lid. She held the jar out for me to see. The powder inside was dark and sparkly. Glitter-dirt, was my first thought.

But I was fairly certain Blue's special ingredient wasn't dirt.

"Take a whiff of this," Blue said. "Tell me what you smell."

The powder had a sweet, spicy aroma to it. "Cinnamon?" I asked.

"Nope." Blue shook her head. "Guess again."

"Something . . . spicy. Cayenne?"

"Good guess, but no." Blue grinned. "This jar contains the rarest and most wonderful of all ingredients you will ever cook with, Emma Pearl: pure, undiluted hope."

Blue pinched a small amount from the jar and snapped the dust in the batch of Boneyard Brew. When hope hit the surface, the whole cauldron bubbled and sparkled.

"What's it really?" I asked.

"Hope!" Blue said again. "You stir while I tell you the tale. Many years ago, when we were young idiots instead of old idiots, Club Pancake took a road trip to the World's Fair. I don't suppose they have the World's Fair anymore. But the World's Fair was a big to-do for many decades. You saw new inventions, fine contraptions, thinkers, and dreamers, and all kinds of crazy food. I ventured down one of the food aisles and saw a funny-looking booth with colored flags rippling from the tent poles. A little man stood on an old chair in front of the booth. He played a jaunty tune on his mandolin. He had one of those long mustaches, the kind that swirl at the ends. And he was peddling little unmarked jars of spices. Well, I picked up one of the jars and, as soon as I did, the music stopped. The little man touched my arm and asked me a question."

"What'd he say?" I asked, stirring the brew slowly.

"He grinned up at me and said . . . 'Do you truly believe that anything is possible?' "

"What'd you tell him?"

"I told him the truth." Blue smiled. "I said, 'Absolutely!' The little man handed me this jar. He said once every ten years—on the coldest night of the year—stardust falls on top of Mount Mitchell. That'd be a miracle in itself, the ability to catch and keep falling stardust. Takes years to learn how to harvest stardust properly. But the stardust on that mountain comes from the North Star—the wishing star. He collected the stardust so carefully, he said, sifting through snow with his bare hands for tiny wish particles that glowed in the moonlight. Do you know how much hope rests on the wishing star, Emma Pearl?"

I shook my head.

"Enough for a lifetime," Blue said. "Just a pinch of wishing stardust in someone's drink fills them with hope, no matter how sad their days have been. It doesn't just work on people, either. A pinch of wishing stardust over a dried-up garden makes it bloom bright."

I looked down at the contents of the jar. "And so you sprinkled it in hot cocoa?"

Blue nodded. "I did. Because people need hope. You'd be amazed at what a person can do with just a pinch of it."

"If we have so much hope in the hot cocoa, why are we ever sad?" I asked.

"It took many years for me to see that hope doesn't take sadness away," Blue said sincerely. "But hope reminds you there's something good in spite of the sadness. There's joy still ahead, still yours for the taking."

That's one thing I've always loved about my granny. Regardless of my age, and the fact that I'm small for my age, she's never been one for baby talk.

"You said it took a long time for you to figure that out. How come?"

Blue took over stirring for a while as she mixed in another spiral of glitter. "I had my Destiny Dream when I was twenty years old, Emma. I dreamed of boxing gloves in my field of blue flowers. I'd already set my sights on becoming a professional boxer at that point in my life. So the dream was just affirmation for me. I would win the women's boxing championship of the world."

I hopped up on the nearest counter. "You *were* a famous boxer."

"But I wasn't a *winning* boxer." Blue smiled at me. "I traveled from state to state. I'd fight. Sometimes, I'd win. But every time the championship rolled around, I lost. And I'd get letters from home about how my mama was sick and wanted to see me. About how Periwinkle missed me like crazy. I thought they didn't understand. I was fighting for them. If I could just win the prize money boxing . . . they'd be set for life. We wouldn't have to depend on this cafe. Lord knows it's never been easy to keep this place up. So I kept fighting. That's when these happened . . ." Blue traced her finger down one of her flower tattoos, an iris with purple petals.

"You got your first tattoo?"

Blue nodded. "I got a flower for every state I passed through in my boxing days. But I got flowers for . . . other reasons, too. This iris on my forearm, it's the state flower of Tennessee, of course. But I remembered the irises that grew down at the general store where Peri and I ate candy bars on Friday nights."

She pointed to a cluster of blue flowers around her wrist. "These reminded me of the forget-me-nots that bloom in Blackbird Hollow. That's where my friends were. And I wanted to know they were always with me. Every flower on my arm has a meaning: Hope. Joy. Love. Patience. I guess I wanted permanent reminders that it's possible to bloom, even when you feel defeated. I finally gave up fighting. Came back home, penniless. Mama and Club Pancake were waiting for me at the door with hot cocoa. Hot cocoa with a pinch of hope inside."

Blue grinned as she stretched her arm out to me. I traced the red rose inked on her forearm. "That was my last tattoo," she said wistfully. "A red rose for true love. I got it when I met your grandfather."

She left the brew simmering while she traced the tattoo with her own hand. The lines around her eyes deepened. I've heard laughter is responsible for the lines on our faces as we age. And I hope that's true. But I knew so many of Blue's lines had come from sorrow.

"I didn't have him in my life for long," she said. "And I went through . . . a dark spell when he passed on. Even then, Club Pancake was there for me, sprinkling hope in my brew. I did the same for them, many times."

I nodded. "Topher would do that for me, too. And Cody Belle. And you."

Blue nodded. "We're lucky, you and me. To have people who love us more than wishing stars."

She continued stirring as she talked. "I remember your grandfather's last year on earth. I knew he wouldn't be here long, you see. Some weeks, I felt numb. Like it was impossible to feel again. You know what that's like."

I nodded.

"It was Greta and Periwinkle who pulled me out of my slump. Periwinkle bought me a brand-new jukebox full of new songs. And Greta took over making big cauldrons of hot cocoa. We'd closed the cafe to the public that night. We danced up the dust of days gone by. We drank the stuff that dreams are made of. Your mama was a little girl back then. She danced, too. She loved the cafe even when she was little. Just like you. You remind me so much of her."

I looked down at my shoelaces through a soft haze of tears.

Blue cleared her throat. "I don't know what's really in there. For all I know, I could be sprinkling dirt in everybody's brew." Blue chuckled. "But I think the little man with the long mustache was onto something. I think he found a wishing star. And if the day comes when I run out of stardust, I still have my friends. I still have you and Topher. So I'm never empty on hope."

I hopped off the counter and leaned my head against Blue's arm. "You did fulfill your destiny, Blue. You fight battles for your friends all the time. You never stop fighting for people you love. That's a mighty legacy."

Blue shrugged. "I . . . never thought of it that way. Go on," she said. "It's a Gypsy Rose summer. The day's almost done. Go spend the rest of it with your friends."

I threw my arms around Blue's waist. "I am spending it with my friend."

Granny Blue, my faithful fighter, wrapped her strong arms around me. She hugged me tight.

The cafe floors shook as folks danced around the room, clapping and stomping to the beat of the music. I sat at my corner table, paging through the Book of Days, while I drank a mug of brew. I had to be close to finding the treasure. Neither the unsigned contract nor the gas-guzzling dump truck presently squashing the iris blooms could convince me otherwise.

I just wished Cody Belle and Earl were there to help me. And neither of them had shown up. The Wildflowers had given me tons of inspiration and good ideas over the past few years. But they weren't living, breathing, talking friends who could help me find the treasure.

Alice started thumping the guitar as Mr. Marcum joined in on the old piano. People danced the same as they always did. But a good-bye kind of sadness had settled over us. I know I'm lucky to have a place in the world so special I never want to leave it. But that doesn't make the letting go any easier.

The one familiar sound I did not hear was my brother's violin. I figured he was still busy chasing Waverly Valentine down the streets of Blackbird Hollow. But then I felt a slight tap on my shoulder and turned to see Topher standing behind me in a button-up shirt and Levi's.

"Care to dance?" asked my big brother.

"I don't dance anymore. You know that."

"Not even with me?" He pulled out the chair and sat down beside me. "How can I change your mind?"

"I'll dance," I said, "IF . . . you tell me how you know Waverly Valentine."

Topher looked down at the lines on the table, concentrating carefully. "Remember last summer? When I worked as a chef at Hidden Ridge?"

"Yes. I remember I missed you like crazy." Hidden Ridge was a camp at the top of Huckleberry Mountain. Only the most hard-core hikers make it to the top of Huckleberry. Once they get there, cabins and real bathrooms and even a small cafeteria are waiting. Topher decided to spend a few weeks there last summer, cooking above the clouds.

"That's where I met Waverly," he told me. "And we hit it off . . . right away. She was game for trying every weird muffin combination I baked."

I nodded. "The girl knows her baked goods."

"And she was just . . . different. She was smart and funny and weird in a good way. So bossy and awesome."

"She's a wonderful kind of pretty. Topher . . . did you break her heart?"

Topher sighed. Nodded. I punched him hard in the arm.

"I didn't mean to!" he said. "I was scared, I guess. It seems like a dumb excuse now. But I was thinking so much about Mama that summer. It'd been a while since she'd gone. But it's like it was all crashing against me then. And my heart was a mess. I tried, though. I even wrote a song for Waverly on my violin. I asked her to meet me the next day, so I could play it for her. But then I got scared and . . . I never showed up. I hiked back down the mountain and figured I'd never see her again. I thought of her every day, though."

"Obviously somebody wants you two to reconnect." I grinned.

"I'm trying," he said. "But she's still not talking to me much. So!" He clapped his hands. "That brings me back to you. It's time to dance again, Emma Pearl. Mom would say the same thing if she was here."

Topher was right. She would say that. She'd pull me out on the floor herself and spin me around.

So, for the first time in years, I stood up and walked to the middle of the cafe with my brother. "Darlin' Daisy" was already on its third time through.

"Do-si-do through the windy forest,
Write your name on the tall oak tree,
Catch a little star,

Put it in your pocket,
But don't forget to wait for me."

I tried to dance. I really did. We spun in circles. But even though my feet were moving, they felt heavier with every step. Because my heart felt heavy. You'd think the Big Empty wouldn't weigh a person down so much, but it does.

Suddenly, I was still and Topher was kneeling down in front of me. "What's wrong?"

People danced in a blur all around us. Music was rising up on invisible wings, the same as always, flying and floating and filling the air with energy. But I still felt lost.

The Boneyard would belong to Warren Steele as soon as Blue signed the papers.

I didn't understand my extraordinary destiny.

My mama would still be gone. Really gone. I wouldn't be connected to her at all.

I wrapped my arms around Topher's shoulders and whispered, "I don't remember her voice sometimes. We used to make up songs every day after school. We weren't finished, you know?"

Topher locked his arms tight around me, the way older brothers do best. I didn't just feel steadier, I felt stronger. Like nobody in the world could bother me or pick on me. Not today. Not then. Not when he was there.

"I have an idea," he said, pulling back to smile at me. "Come with me."

Topher grabbed my hand and we ran for the back porch, the place that used to be my Fortress of Wonder. I didn't hang out back there anymore. There were no twinkly lights now. No woodland treasures.

"Don't go anywhere," Topher said as he scrambled back inside. He returned with his arms full of Topher stuff: three folding chairs, two buckets, drumsticks, his violin, and a laptop. Waiting tables for so many years really does wonders for balance. Topher situated the laptop on one of the chairs. Then he pulled out another folding chair and said, "Have a seat." He plopped an upturned bucket in front of me, and crisscrossed my drumsticks across the top. He unfolded his own chair near the computer.

Finally, he took his fiddle and perched across from me.

"Your idea is a jam session? That's not exactly new," I said.

"Patience, Miss Casey. Now, as you know, Mom considered herself a mountain music purist. She said her music was only meant to be experienced live, loud, and free."

I nodded. "I know. She refused to do any recordings. That's why we don't have an album."

"That's what she thought," Topher said, with a twinkle of excitement in his eye. "But Mom had a big following. So

I figured somebody out there snuck in and recorded her singing. And I was right. I found a bootleg copy."

Topher leaned toward the computer. With a swift click, scratchy music notes drifted through the speakers. Soft guitar music filled the air.

And then came a sweet, raspy voice that my heart recognized . . . a voice I was afraid I'd forgotten.

I gasped. I looked at my brother. "Is that . . . Mom?"

He nodded.

At first, I just listened, and I wiped the tears off my face. I closed my eyes and let her song fall over me sweetly, calling out to the remembering place in me.

Maybe my life would never be whole without her in it.

But for the first time I could remember, I found joy in thinking about her again, and not just sadness.

I listened to the way she sang.

The way she strummed.

"Shall we join in?" Topher asked, tucking his fiddle beneath his chin.

And soon I was tapping out a rhythm on the old bucket, and it sounded like:
summer nights
and firefly skies,
and the rumble of an old Harley-Davidson;
screen doors slamming shut,

Blue's laugh,

Mom's voice,

her songs,

wishing stars,

and a wild, glorious wind whistling through the midnight sky.

I played along with a song I loved. I sang along with the voice I missed, the voice I'd never forget. The laughter of the people I love . . . that's the best music in the world.

Finally, the song popped and crackled to a stop. I looked over my brother's shoulder and realized Waverly Valentine was standing in the doorway.

"Are you okay?" Waverly asked softly. At the sound of her voice, Topher spun up out of his seat, nearly tripping over the record player to get to her.

"Waverly." He whispered her name.

"You." She jabbed her finger against his chest so he couldn't get too close. "I will talk to you. For five minutes, and that's it." And then she turned her attention back to me. "Lovely to see you, Emma. As always."

I saluted Waverly with my drumsticks as she walked away.

"No pressure," I said to my brother. "But don't mess this up again."

"Thanks," he mumbled as he marched after his not-so-long-lost love.

As I cleaned up the Fortress of Wonder, I realized I'd left my messenger bag under the tall oak tree. I'd left my stuff in the graveyard more than a few times, but I didn't want Warren Steele's people accidentally tossing it in a dumpster.

As I stepped into the graveyard, storm clouds were huddled together as far as I could see. I figured it was the sight of the coming storm that made Earl want to get home. Maybe he had that same feeling I did; the coming storm would be a doozy. I ran up the hill where I'd left my stuff. I sat under the tree again and checked my bag. The Book of Days was still safe. So was the old hymnal.

As I thumbed through the fragile pages, it occurred to me that every book in the world is somebody's Book of Days. Some books are so special that you never forget where you were the first time you read them. The same was true with the hymnal, I figured. What worries pressed on a person's heart when they read those words? And when they opened it all those years ago, did they remember a song that had carried them through a season of sorrow? Or joy? It's magical to me, the way memories hide in music.

I turned the page . . . and found a bloom from a Telling Vine. The flower was white, and smooth as silk. It didn't look faded like the pages. It looked as new as the blooms on the farm. The Keeping Susans had preserved it, I suppose.

I held the bloom in the palm of my hand, and stroked the flower petals as gently as if they were wings.

Granny Blue believes there is always a still moment before a storm, a strange moment of calm before the air all around you turns to chaos. Somehow, I knew that moment was exactly the same way for me. The air around me seemed so still, so quiet that I could hear my own breath, my heartbeat. My fingertips tingled in anticipation, even though I was only holding a flower. My neck prickled . . . the same way it had when I first heard the Conductor.

Maybe someone had simply pressed the flower into a book and buried it. That's the conclusion I came to in my head.

But my heart came up with another idea: Maybe someone had taken great pains to hide the flower.

A cool breeze swept through the cemetery.

I lifted the flower close to my ear, even though I didn't have to do that. The message in the bloom was loud and clear . . . sung out in the strong voice of a child.

I knew that voice. I'd heard it in the cemetery before . . .

"Beneath the stars of Blackbird Hollow
By the shadows of the ridge
Down a path no man can follow

Is the treasure that we hid—
So, Darlin' Daisy, lace your boots up,
Take the lantern, shine it bright,
Oh, these summer days are dwindling,
But we're going to dance tonight . . ."

The two songs were sung together with no pause, as if they'd been connected all along. The song I knew belonged to the Conductor—and Darlin' Daisy. They folded together into one song.

I suddenly felt like the world's dumbest treasure hunter. We didn't just have starry skies in Blackbird Hollow, Tennessee. And we didn't just have stardust in our hot chocolate.

We had stars in the floors, stars we danced over and around nearly every day.

The treasure was down a path no man could follow because it wasn't a map. It was in the song.

And if I was right, it was underneath the floor. I'd been walking over it all along.

❀ ❦ ❁

I raced back to the cafe to find it empty. It was as if everybody'd magically disappeared. Blue was gone. The musicians had left their instruments propped in chairs. Had Warren Steele evicted everybody on a moment's notice?

"Hello!" I yelled out. "Where is everybody?"

Blue'd left a note on the counter near a fresh muffin batch:

Emma,
CALL ASAP
—Granny B

I'd call Blue soon, all right. I would call her with *great* news.

Bear scampered down the stairs from our apartment and nuzzled against my leg. I scooped her up into my arms and kissed her ear. "Stay close to me, okay? Help me be brave?"

Bear licked my face.

I settled her down on the ground and double-checked to make sure my flashlight was working, in case the storm zapped the power. With the bag slung over my shoulder, I walked through the back door of the pantry, down into the cellar. Bear followed me down the creaky steps. Even though the sound of her paws was only a tiny thump-thump-thump, I felt brave knowing she was there. Once we were in the middle of the cellar, I looked up. Dim light shone down through the holes in the cafe's floor, just like stars.

"These stars have been here forever," I told Bear as I

picked her up and held her close. "If the treasure was down here, we would have found it . . . right?"

I circled the flashlight around and saw dusty footprints on the floors. I followed them to the far corner of the cafe, where a shelf of fruity jams had been pushed away. A pile of boards lay scattered on the floor. The lock on a door had been broken, and the door pushed open . . . and there was only darkness behind it.

Someone had just walked in there.

Someone else was looking for the treasure.

"Fear is just a flashlight that helps you find your courage," I whispered. "Stay, Bear." I could tell Bear didn't want to stay, but she did. And I knew she would faithfully wait until I came back. If I came back.

I pointed my light into the darkness, and stepped into the cave.

Until then, I didn't know the basement of the Boneyard Cafe was connected to the caves beneath Blackbird Hollow. I guess Blue knew about it, but she'd never seen it as a fact worth mentioning, probably because she knew I'd go explore. I'd seen other entrances to the caves on field trips when I was a kid, but I forgot how far they stretched. They ran like vines beneath our town, deep into the mountains and woods.

I walked slowly into the darkness, keeping the light steady ahead of me.

"Hello?" I finally called out. Only my echo answered at first. And then I heard something up ahead.

"Who's there?" My light trembled against the darkness. And as my light drifted over the far wall of the cave, I saw something in the shadows . . . something like an old box.

Something like a trunk.

Click. Another flashlight beam pierced the darkness, shining over the same box.

"What is that?" The voice sounded like it belonged to an old man, but I didn't take any further time to ponder who it might be.

"It's mine!" I yelled, breaking into a run. My fear drained away, leaving only burning determination.

"Who said that?!" the voice yelled.

My flashlight flickered and wavered as I ran for the old trunk. When I was close enough, I jumped and stretched out my arms, supergirl-style.

My light shattered to the ground just as I fell onto the trunk, trying to pull it close to me.

"I'll protect it!" I yelled.

A cool wind blew through the caves.

"Get away from the ridge . . ." came a whisper from above us.

CHAPTER SIXTEEN

The other intruder pointed his flashlight above us but there was no need: I recognized the squawky voice. "Be careful, Penny Lane!" I yelled.

The bird flapped down onto the corner of the trunk. "I'll put your keys in the fridge," Penny Lane squeaked. Despite my circumstances, I nearly smiled in disbelief. But I had to focus on the task at hand.

"You okay there?" came an old man's voice. He shone the flashlight in my face. "It's not safe down here in the caves."

As I squinted into the light, I could make out some of his features. He was the guy with tired eyes from the survey team, the boss with the hard hat. "That trunk looks pretty old," he said. The hope in his voice was unmistakable. "Is it locked?"

I nodded, reaching my arms across the trunk. Not only was the trunk old, but it was big and bulky and not exactly made for cuddling. Still, I tried to hug the thing as close to me as I could.

The man waved his flashlight around the floor of the cave. "You didn't happen to see a key lying around, did you?"

A key. I shivered at the thought of it. I hadn't seen a key lying around the cave anywhere. But I'd seen one in my dreams, tucked into a bouquet of flowers. It's sad I couldn't keep the key hidden in my mind until I needed it, then pull it free of my imagination and unlock the trunk later. When I was safe. When the treasure was safe.

"No . . ." I told the man. "I'm sure the key's been gone a long time. Which is a good thing, because I have to keep this safe from . . . someone."

The man raised his fuzzy eyebrows. "Who?"

"Some jerk who wants to turn my entire town into a parking lot," I said, gripping the trunk edges so tight my fingers hurt. "He wants to turn *my home* and my grave-yard into a parking lot, too."

Penny Lane's bird-feet tapped against the trunk as she walked across the dusty surface. "I'LL PUT YOUR KEYS IN THE FRIDGE!"

The old man looked at the bird. "Not the first time somebody's said that to me this week."

I hugged the trunk closer as a cold realization came over me.

"Yep," he said, handing me my flashlight. "I'm Warren Steele."

I never imagined Warren Steele looking like a normal person, like somebody who'd laugh at a joke or take his grandkids out for ice cream.

"Not what you imagined, am I?" he said, as if he could read my mind. "I know Blue filled your head with images of Warren the greedy dirtbag, the big-money man out to crush a town. But someday you'll see that I'm not the villain you think I am. This town is dying. We need to start over."

He shined the flashlight over the roof of the cave. "This town's only ever talked about what *has been*. We'll never move on until we bury the past for good. There's a whole world of opportunity up there."

I raised my eyebrow at him. "If you're so interested in what's happening up there, what are you doing down here in the caves?"

Warren's mouth pressed into a flat, angry line. His voice was so low it sent shivers down my arms. "I've been looking for this treasure much longer than you have. It's mine."

My first instinct was to cower. Warren was bigger than me. He was more powerful than me. But I thought about the fire I'd seen in Granny Blue's eyes—and in my mother's eyes—when they stood up for what they believed in. I thought about how it felt to stand my ground against Beretta in the woods. Some bullies never grow up, I realized. "No way," I told him. "I found it first."

"What would a little girl use the money for?" Warren smirked. "I'd put it to good use."

"This *little girl* will use it to preserve a national treasure for years to come."

Warren sniggered. "Preserve?" He shook his head. "Sorry, kid. My men are on their way. They'll help me haul this trunk to the surface, and then it'll be my property. Finders keepers."

"But I found it!" I felt my face getting hotter. "I'll tell them you stole it from me."

"EMMA!" Cody Belle yelled from the entrance to the cave. "EMMA!"

I shone my light out into the darkness. "That's my light, Cody Belle!" I hollered. "Walk toward it. Warren Steele's back here, too, but I have him cornered."

Warren rolled his eyes and tried using his walkie-talkie. But the only response he got was full-static.

"Emma!" Cody Belle did not walk toward the light; she ran full blast and slid at me, throwing her arms around my neck.

"Are you okay?" I asked her.

"No! Everybody's freaking out. Earl's mom said he never made it home from the woods today. Have you seen him? It's raining really hard now."

"What?" My volcanic anger toward Warren Steele shifted into a much more terrible feeling: worry. "Earl had plenty of time to get home."

Didn't he?

I didn't have my drumsticks with me, but a scary rhythm pounded against my heart.

Thunder. Lightning. Endless rain. The storm was getting worse.

Soaked jeans sliding through mud and muck. Earl might have crawled under his house, to his sanctuary. He was afraid of mighty winds. I was more worried about a raging flood.

Silence. Scary, awful silence. Earl couldn't call for help.

Only one person knew where his sanctuary was. Me.

Warren Steele had rested his hand on the trunk, oblivious to what was happening. I loosened my grip . . . on the trunk, and on my destiny. I knew what I had to do. If something happened to Earl, I'd never forgive myself. Walking away would mean I'd leave a big hole in the Book of Days . . .

Still, I knew my mom would understand.

Love above everything; that's the choice she would have made.

"Let's go," I said, standing up and reaching for Cody Belle.

Warren shoved his useless walkie-talkie into its holster. "Come to your senses?" he asked me.

"My treasure's not in that box," I said with a catch in my voice. I'd found the Conductor's treasure. And now I was giving it away. All along, untold riches had been beneath the floor of the cafe. But in the moment Cody Belle told me Earl was missing, I came to an important conclusion: My treasures weren't just in the walls of that place. My treasure was the people I loved.

Earl had nothing to do with a key or with saving my home. But he was a treasure to me. Even as I stepped away from my destiny, I felt the Wildflowers cheering me on.

I grabbed Cody Belle's hand and ran for the entrance of the cave. We ran back through the cellar, up the stairs to the kitchen, and then burst outside into the pouring rain.

The thunder boomed, but I didn't shiver. Lightning swiped across the skies, but I didn't try to hide. I held on tight to my best friend, and we ran.

My lungs ached.

The muscles in my legs burned.

Hold tight, Earl! I was too winded to yell the words, but I wished them. Hoped them. Prayed them. *Please, Earl. Please hold tight . . .*

CHAPTER SEVENTEEN

The Chance house was located down a muddy hillside, and sat flush against the woods. Just as I feared, the rainwater had pooled down around the house and the porch, already knee-deep.

I scampered down the slippery slope, falling and sliding all the way down.

"Be careful!" I heard Cody Belle call out behind me. I sloshed through the water in Earl's front yard, calling out his name.

It chilled me to think that even if Earl had found his voice, his mom probably wouldn't have heard him call out from under the house. I shined my flashlight under the porch, but didn't see him. I sloshed around to the back of the house and kneeled down again.

The water was rising, but a person could still hide under there if they wanted to. Cody Belle yanked my arm. "You're not crawling under there, are you?"

"Maybe," I yelled. "This is Earl's sanctuary."

I came down on all fours, my knees and hands planting deep in the mud. Cold water covered my wrists. I shivered as I leaned down lower so I could see underneath Earl's house. And I prayed to God no rabid possum would swim out and gouge out my eyeballs.

"Earl," I hollered, "are you in there?"

I knew Earl wouldn't answer me. But I hoped he'd knock against a pipe or something if he was hiding under his own house.

Which, in fact, he was.

Cody Belle held the flashlight steady behind me. Suddenly, her beam shined over Earl's face, and I was so happy I nearly forgot that I was rescuing him.

"Can you follow the light?" I yelled to him. "Can you crawl out?"

Earl didn't move. He sat scrunched up in the corner, clutching a ratty quilt tight against his chest. He shivered, maybe from the cold water beginning to pool around him, but also, maybe, because he was terrified. I remembered the time Blue and I first found Penny Lane hobbling through the woods, flapping her one good wing and squawking because she was scared. She tried to sing, but even her song sounded rusty. Blue held out her arms and talked so easy, in a lullaby voice, until the bird went still and flapped up into her gentle hands. And then we carried Penny out of the woods.

I get that Earl's no bird; he's a boy twice my size. But maybe every creature in the world needs to be reminded that they aren't alone. That somebody cares about them. That they have a friend to lead them out of their present mess.

"Okay," I yelled to Earl. "Plan B! I'm going to crawl under there, and you can follow me out."

"Hold the flashlight steady." I glanced back up at Cody Belle. "I'll be back."

"Promise?" she asked, her shoulders scrunched against the cold rain.

I nodded. "Promise."

"I can see why you selected this spot for contemplation, Earl," I said as I crawled slowly through the rising, murky water underneath the Chance house. The ground dropped off and I slid, going chin-deep in the mud. "It's very quiet and cool under here," I grunted.

This was all a lie, of course. Some sanctuaries and special places are full of a sweet and peaceful darkness. They soothe your soul like a lullaby. The underbelly of Earl's porch was not a lullaby place; it was swampy and abysmal.

I had no clue what he was doing under there, but Earl's a skittish type, so I kept talking to him in a gentle voice, trying to be positive. Finally, I could rise up a bit taller again, even though I was still on all fours. I crawled to Earl's corner.

"Okay, Earl!" I said. "You and me, we're going to crawl in that direction. Right into the light. Okay?"

Earl blinked down at the bundle in his arms. From far back, I thought Earl was holding a lumpy quilt or something. But now, I realized Earl was hugging a sweet old dog.

"You have a golden retriever!" I said, reaching out to pet the dog's velvety ears. Earl's dog wasn't shivering; he just stuck close beside his buddy, strong and sweet. If people were as nice as dogs, the world would be a much better place. I patted the soft fur on the dog's forehead. "Earl, you might be too scared to get out from under here yourself. But you can be brave for your dog, right? We have to get the dog out."

Cody Belle yelled, "What's taking so long? HURRY!"

"We're coming!" I said as a loud burst of thunder rippled overhead. Earl's breath caught. The dog rested its head on Earl's shoulder. The water was steadily rising.

"Earl," I said earnestly. "All you have to do is swivel around and scoot backward. You can keep your eye on the dog and on me. And I'll get us out of here, easy as pie. Just pretend we're swimming, okay? Let's go!"

I don't know if Earl would have jumped into action if his dog hadn't cooperated so thoughtfully. But the dog was more than ready to get out of that swamp and so was I. Earl turned around, scooting backward into the light. The dog crawled between us, keeping his eyes on Earl. I was our flood caboose, crawling along behind the dog, hoping and praying and wishing we'd get out from under the house before the water got too high.

Cody Belle cheered us on from the outside. "You're nearly here!" she called out.

"We're nearly there—" I meant to echo Cody Belle's affirmation as a way of hurrying Earl along. But I accidentally swallowed a bucketful of muddy water.

I couldn't stand up.

I couldn't crawl forward.

I gagged and coughed, trying to push myself ahead another inch or two. But I couldn't feel anybody close to me anymore.

Suddenly, the light was very near. I felt a strong hand reach out and pull me free from the slimy water under Earl's house.

"Emma!" It was a voice I didn't recognize.

I fell down on my knees and coughed up all the water stuck inside me. And then I glanced toward the person who'd just spoken. Cody Belle was staring at him, too, her eyes wide in disbelief.

Earl touched his throat. He said my name again. "Emma . . . are you okay?"

This time, I was the one who couldn't find any words to say. I threw my arms around Earl's neck and hugged him tight.

Somehow, all four of us—me, Cody Belle, Earl, and the dog—finally managed to get inside Earl's house. The storm had zapped the phones and the lights. I tried to text Blue on the Tracking Device, but I wasn't sure I had enough power for the text to go through.

For a flicker of a second, I wondered if I could make it back to the cafe in time to save the treasure. To claim it as mine. I knew I'd made the right choice when I left it behind to help my friend. But walking away forever was hard. The treasure belonged to somebody else now. That realization didn't just make me sad; it made me ache.

Earl brought us towels and flopped down beside me. Seeing him there and healthy gave my heart a happy jolt again. Earl Chance was okay.

He was more than okay.

"So I'm guessing your sanctuary is under the house because of the storm you survived," I said, wiping the mud off my arms. "Do you want to talk about it?"

He nodded. "Do you remember when the tornadoes came last summer?"

Earl's voice matched the kind of person I already knew him to be. Because his voice was kind, and strong. There was a gentleness in the way he spoke, and little moments that reminded me of radio static when his voice would scratch. Probably from not being used for so long.

"I absolutely remember the storm day," I told Earl. It's not the kind of moment you forget. "I've always heard that mountains are supposed to keep tornadoes away. But we've learned differently. Cody Belle and I were at the cafe. We had to hunker down with Blue and Periwinkle in the kitchen."

"So I was staying with my dad when the tornadoes came." Earl swallowed. His shoulders stiffened. Fudge, the dog, jumped up beside Earl and licked him. Earl ran his trembling fingers through the dog's muddy fur. "Dad lived in a trailer. It was a nice trailer, in a nice lot. But mobile homes are dangerous during tornadoes."

Cody Belle nodded. "I was so afraid for my mom and dad. They were both at work, and they were fine. But it's awful because it happens so fast."

Earl nodded. A bead of sweat trickled down his forehead. "My dad was working, too, and I was home alone with Fudge. I knew a bad storm was coming, because Fudge had been whimpering all afternoon, walking around with his tail tucked. And then Dad called and told me to get out of the trailer, to get low in the ditch near my house because a tornado was coming."

"You had to get *out* of the trailer?" I asked, jumping up to get Earl a glass of water. Brew would be better in a time like this, but water would have to do.

"Dad said it was safer than being inside. Before I could ask him why, I realized he was wrong about something. The tornado wasn't *coming*. It was already there."

Earl swept his hand across his forehead. He lowered his voice as he spoke. "Before I even got off the phone, the hair on my arms stood up. Like the room was suddenly full of static electricity, ya know? And then I heard it—"

Earl closed his eyes. His chest heaved with sharp, sudden bursts of breath. I scooted closer to him on the couch, and Cody Belle kneeled down on the floor in front of him.

"You don't have to tell us anything else," I whispered.

Earl shook his head. "I want to tell y'all. I'd always heard people say that a tornado sounds like a train. And it does. But it's more like a train would sound if you're a bug stuck on the tracks and you can't move. It was a roar from the sky, and it was coming right for me. At first, I was so scared I could hardly move. But I didn't want anything to happen to Fudge. So I snapped on his leash and we ran outside."

A tear rolled down Earl's face. He didn't try to wipe it away. "We saw them as soon as we stepped outside—not just one, but two different spirals, dark as smoke spinning through the flat fields near Dad's trailer. They looked evil, like demons dancing out of the sky, ripping up everything they touched. Fudge was howling, but it's like I couldn't move. I watched the tornadoes rip up the Smiths' house. The Davidsons' house. Just smash them into rubble while we stood there. I thought, what if people were in there? What if they didn't get out?"

Earl pressed his face against the soft fur of his dog. "Somehow, I found enough courage to move. I picked up the dog and ran. I mean, Fudge is no lightweight," Earl said with a smile. "But I carried him like he was nothing. We jumped into the ditch, and I held Fudge as tight as I could. And I screamed. I screamed for my dad and my mom, like I was a little kid or something. But they couldn't hear me. Nobody could hear me. I was stuck in a ditch with a tornado getting closer. Everything went dark, and the next thing I remember is people pulling me and Fudge out of the ditch. We were both okay. But my voice was gone. I couldn't talk. Or maybe I didn't want to talk."

Earl looked down at his dog. "Fudge never left my side. But the trailer was gone. I'm still afraid of storms. I want to be as close to the ground as I can. I can't help it."

"Earl," I said, swiveling around where I could see him better. "Consider the facts here. You saved yourself. You saved your dog!" I grinned. "You're a hero."

Earl shook his head. "Not really. Because I'm *still* afraid . . . of lots of things."

"Here's an indisputable fact, Earl: Heroes are afraid." I shrugged. "I know a thing or two about this. I come from a family that's full—and I mean FULL—of brave people. And the one thing they all had in common is that they were afraid when it came down to doing what needed to be done. Maybe there are people in the world who really are fearless. Cody Belle's one of the toughest people I know and she's afraid of stuff."

Cody Belle nodded. "It's true."

"All the brave people I know . . . they're still afraid even when they do brave things. My mom said fear's like a flashlight that helps you find your courage."

Earl smiled. "Your mom sounds like a cool lady."

"She was the coolest," I said proudly. "You know what I realized the other day, when we happened upon the evil woodland creature better known as Beretta Simpson?"

Earl's cheek dimpled. "What?"

"I learned that courage and fear always come as a pair. If you've got one inside you, you've surely got the other. I have a hard time drumming up enough brave for myself. But when it comes to you and Cody Belle, I'd take on the world. We'll just be brave for each other."

"I can do that." He grinned. "I can be brave for y'all."

"Same here." Cody Belle smiled.

"So," I said. "Now that you're talking, want to tell me what you were doing in the graveyard that night?"

"It's going to sound crazy," he said.

"I like crazy," I told him.

"Have you ever had a weird dream, Emma? Not just a strange dream, like the kind that comes when you have a big test the next day or whatever. But a dream that . . . means something. Do you believe in dreams like that?"

Cody Belle's eyes widened as she looked at me for an answer. The Touch feathered against my neck. I shivered as I said, "You have no idea."

He went on. "For a while, I had this crazy idea that the tornado had taken my voice away. Like, hidden it somewhere. And then I dreamed my voice was in the woods near the cemetery. I dreamed about a girl holding a jar, running. It was my voice inside that jar . . . and I had to find it. Instead, I found you screaming at me. And this." He reached under the collar of his shirt and pulled a shoestring necklace over his head. He handed the necklace to me. "I found it near the woods. My flashlight shone over the brass part there and I knew . . . I just knew it was special."

Even before I opened my hand, I knew what I was holding. Something metal and cold. Something with a strange, swirly design in the center.

Something I'd only dreamed about.

Earl had found the key.

CHAPTER EIGHTEEN

We arrived back at the cafe just as Warren's minions were carrying the trunk out of the caves and into the dining area. Because the trunk was so heavy, Warren had to wait for several of his men to come and move it. They'd tracked mud and dust all over the floor of the cafe, which didn't surprise me. Of course they didn't care about the cafe. To them, it was one more place to be demolished. To me, it was everything. The restaurant was still empty, probably because people were looking for Earl. Penny Lane swooped in circles around Warren Steele's head, occasionally diving at him. This wasn't really helping anything, but I appreciated Penny's loyalty.

Earl saw the treasure trunk and grabbed my arm. "Emma! He has the treasure!"

"I know." I glared at Warren.

Warren saw me and groaned. "I thought you were gone."

"I was hoping *you* were gone."

"Wait." Earl looked down at me. "Does that mean you were already here?"

"*I'LL PUT YOUR KEYS IN THE FRIDGE,*" Penny squawked at Warren.

Warren waved the bird away and yelled out for one of his men. "Bring me a crowbar from the truck!"

"A crowbar?" I gasped. "That treasure is hundreds of years old. You'll damage it!"

"Sweetheart," Warren said as his men dropped the heavy trunk with a loud THUNK. "Gold is the only thing I've ever known that can't be damaged."

Earl looked down at me. "Emma . . . you left it? You walked away from the buried treasure?!"

"I made the decision to walk away," I clarified. As Warren raised the crowbar to pop the lock, I cried out for him to stop. I took the key from my neck and handed it over.

"At least be careful with it," I said softly.

"How about that." Warren held the strange old key in his hand for a moment. Then he clutched it in his fist. "I've waited my whole life for this treasure."

"Me, too," I said sadly.

I'm sorry, Lily Kate, I thought to myself. *I'm sorry, Mom.*

Earl reached out and took my hand in his.

The electricity was still out, even though the storm had

subsided. One of Warren's goons tilted a flashlight over the lock. "Go ahead, boss."

"You should let Emma open that," Earl said. "Haven't you heard the legend? The Conductor only leads the pure of heart to the treasure. If anybody else tries to open that . . ." Earl shook his head. "Things could get weird."

I could see by the look in Warren's eyes that he was a bit more superstitious than he'd let on.

He shrugged. "If the little girl wants to open it, that's fine."

He tossed me the key.

I kneeled down in front of the box while Warren's men held flashlights over the treasure. I pushed the key into the lock and heard the satisfying click.

"Untold riches," Warren Steele murmured happily. I had a feeling his imagination was full of shopping centers and fancy fountains, golf courses and touristy stuff.

Untold riches. I imagined the Boneyard Cafe in business for years to come. I imagined closed shops on Main Street reopening. I imagined the graveyard spruced up, sacred and beautiful again. I imagined my name in the Book of Days, right behind my mom's name.

It was official: I was my family's biggest failure.

"Open it!" Warren barked.

"Leave her alone!" Cody Belle shined her light in his eyes. "It's Emma's, anyway. She found it first!"

While Warren bickered with Cody Belle, I pulled the lock free from the trunk. The lid gave off a loud screech as I pushed it open.

The room fell silent as we stared inside and found . . .

"Flowers," I said.

"More Keeping Susans?" Cody Belle leaned down beside me and took a papery bloom in her hand.

"Flowers?" Warren seethed. He grabbed a handful of flowers from the trunk. He crushed them slowly in his hand, and they scattered to the floor.

"And another book," I said as I ruffled through the flowers. I get it; every book is somebody's treasure. But what was up with people in this town burying *books*?

"Maybe the money is in the book," Warren said, yanking it from my hands.

"Careful!" I jumped up and readied myself to grab the book. But I didn't have to grab it. Warren let the book fall to the floor. He looked down at the book and the trunk full of flowers and shook his head. "Turns out the treasure's a pile of lies, like everything else in this town. Looks like it's yours to keep, my dear. Tell your granny I'll be back in a few hours for that contract."

He stomped out of the cafe, his men scampering along close behind him.

I sat down on the floor again and pulled the book into my lap. My weary band of treasure hunters settled in beside me. Penny Lane perched on the trunk. I turned the cover to reveal an old photograph.

It was a black-and-white photo of a family standing in front of a small house. Even though the photo had no color, my eye went to the sky behind them. It took up every piece of empty space, so much sky you'd never get tired of it. Earl and I turned the pages carefully, looking at more photographs of faces. Of families. And then, on a page by itself, three flowers I'd seen in my dreams:

A daisy.

A violet.

A red rose.

On the next page, tucked into the middle of the book, we found a letter.

"You read it," Earl said.

Here lies the true account of my beloved sister,

Lily Kate Abernathy

The Conductor

CHAPTER NINETEEN

My voice trembled as I read aloud the letter inside.

Here lies the true account of my beloved sister,

Lily Kate Abernathy
The Conductor

Written by Amelia Abernathy

My eyes are old now; the light around me is fading. I can no longer tell a tree from its shadows. The birds look as dark as the night that turned them loose. In these last days, while I can still see the words I lay down on paper, I must tell our story.

In spring of 1860, my sister, Lily Kate Abernathy, had the Destiny Dream of our ancestors. In her field of blue flowers, Lily Kate saw a treasure chest. But there was no *crown or coin or ruby inside. She only saw words painted in the slats of the trunk:*

"For where your treasure is, there will your heart be also."

As is often the case for the destined, it took time for Lily Kate to figure out what her dream meant.

All too soon, it became clear. And we began the most dangerous summer of our lives. We hid treasure in the hills of Blackbird Hollow.

"Keep reading," Earl said as he settled in beside me, holding the flashlight steady.

Before we became conductors, we were flower girls. We set up our flower cart on Main Street, and sold blooms and bouquets to people in the Hollow. The most popular flowers were Starblooms, of course. We sold fresh bundles to midwives and doctors. We sold pouches of crushed Starblooms to travelers to keep in their pockets for any sickness they might encounter. Lily Kate always wore a vial of crushed Starblooms around her neck. My sister was born with a weak heart, according to the doctor. Sometimes the Healing Blues would help her breathe easy and calm down. Since she had a weak heart, maybe she would have died anyway, even if she hadn't given the vial away. I'll always wonder.

For many years, life here in the Hollow was peaceful bliss—full of flowers and music and dances at the church, where our dad was pastor. But then a certain darkness seemed to creep over the Hollow: dark clouds, long shadows, strange whispers of a coming war. Some of the flowers, especially the healing blue Starblooms, withered. Late one night, by the small, brave light of our old lantern, our daddy told us about the Underground Railroad. About how he planned to hide people under the church.

"I think we're alive at this time in history for this reason," Daddy said to us. "Remember, girls, we're not the brave ones. We're giving the brave ones a sanctuary. They are the treasure," he said. "And we must keep them secret."

Lily Kate had already written her dream in the Book of Days. Instead of completing her entry, she ripped out the page, so we could keep our work secret. And so we became conductors, leading the enslaved out of the woods and into the sanctuary of the caves beneath the church. When it was safe, we led them to the river, to press on to their promised land of freedom.

There were others in town who offered up their homes for hiding places. We knew them by the flowers they pinned to their collars or hats:

A violet,

A daisy,

A single red rose.

Safe houses were marked with a discreet symbol—a compass rose—carved somewhere near the door.

Lily Kate made up ghost stories about the graveyard, to keep people from snooping near the church.

The song was my idea. "Darlin' Daisy" marked every safe spot in our town.

The goal was always to get folks to the church. We could hide them for days in the caves connected to the basement. And Daddy drilled stars into the floor to let fresh air, light, and music down into that darkness. For months, we went undetected.

But one night, we were found out. Authorities came to Blackbird Hollow, looking for runaway slaves.

Lily Kate met me in the woods with the family—the treasure—and tucked a Telling Vine into the pocket of my apron. "Move quickly," she told me. "Be quiet as little mice. Get to the other side of the river."

It wasn't until she was gone that I realized she'd given her vial of Starblooms to the little boy. Once I got them safely across the river, I ran back to the church. That's when we found Lily Kate. I remember the doctor telling us that her heart was weak, that it finally gave out. It's a miracle, then, that a weak heart could hold so much joy, so much courage, so much life.

It wasn't until the week after her funeral that I remembered the Telling Vine she'd tucked into my pocket. She'd left a song there that she made up for me—when we walked home hand in hand, when we pushed the flower cart through the misty morning fog. It was as if she knew her time was short, and she wanted me to have a lullaby to keep forever.

I carried on, in secret, with my sister's work. Now I have written an account of our adventures because I know this: Every lifetime, no matter how long it lasts, is a gift. And to love, and be loved, even by one person during your lifetime . . . that is a treasure no one can take from you.

"They were conductors on the Underground Railroad," I said, turning the page. "People were the treasure."

The final page of the book was a photograph of Lily Kate and Amelia Abernathy, standing beside their flower cart, hand in hand. Lily Kate wore an elaborate crown of flowers in her hair. Amelia wore a daisy tucked into her braid, like me.

The silence that filled the room then wasn't awkward or uncomfortable. It was a sweet silence, sacred, even. The rising sun shimmered through the stained-glass window, sending warm, multicolored patches of light over our faces.

Suddenly, the door was flung open and my brother ran inside. "Emma!"

"I'm here!" I yelled back.

"Thank goodness." Topher swooped me up off the ground and hugged me. "They're here!" he yelled over his shoulder. "Are you all okay? Are you hurt? Why are you covered in mud?"

"They came looking for me," Earl offered. "And they found me."

Just as Topher realized an old treasure chest was in the middle of the floor, Waverly Valentine burst into the room.

"Topher!"

Topher gave her a thumbs-up. "They're okay."

"Awesome." Waverly beamed. "Everybody get out here quick. Something strange is happening in the graveyard."

CHAPTER TWENTY

Cody Belle, Earl, and I ran out into the graveyard, with Topher close behind us.

"Emma!" Granny Blue hugged me tight.

"I'll explain later," I told her. "I'm sorry I didn't tell you where I was going."

"*Shh,*" Uncle Peri whispered as he came up to us. "Look . . ."

I opened my eyes to see a bunch of gob-smacked faces. It wouldn't surprise me if the entire town ended up in the graveyard that morning. They'd all probably met up to go looking for Earl Chance. People stood among the graves staring at the ground . . . amazed.

Tiny blue flowers—the same flowers I'd seen blooming on Lily Kate's grave—were blooming everywhere. And in the early morning light, each petal sparkled as though it'd been dunked in glitter. Even as we watched, flowers bloomed out of the ground and around the bases of trees. Flowers even bloomed through the moss on some of the graves. More still bloomed like blue dewdrops off the vines in the maple trees.

"Healing Blues," Aunt Greta said. She stood up from her scooter and hobbled toward the old oak tree. Her hand trembled when she reached for the flower. "They haven't bloomed here in years. Not like this."

Not since the Conductor was here, I thought.

Violets and daisies pushed up through the muddy ground.

Sunflowers bloomed tall, stretching their petals in the morning light. Forget-me-nots covered the ground like party confetti. Gardenias. Magnolias. Morning glory and mountain laurel . . . they all bloomed.

I'd never seen so much color in the graveyard.

The farmers Marcum stood under the tall oak. I saw Mrs. Marcum press her hands against her heart. I ran for her, afraid something was wrong.

But then her husband did the same thing; he rested his hand over his heart.

"I feel it, too . . ." he said. "Or . . . do I *hear* it?"

And then I felt it. *And* heard it. This time the song was slow and beautiful, like a ballad:

"Darlin' Daisy, lace your boots up,
Take the lantern, shine it bright,

Oh, these summer days are dwindling,
But we're going to dance tonight!"

Mr. Marcum was the first to sing along. As other people joined in, the Gypsy Roses began to rain down all around us.

"Darlin' Daisy, pass the schoolhouse,
Creep as quiet as a mouse,
Sneak down Dutch and Vine and Main Streets,
All the way to the old church house.
Sing—

"HALLELUJAH!"

As we shouted, a strange wind came down from the mountains.

I know there is a true and scientific explanation of where the wind comes from. But I like to think it happens when clouds shrug their shoulders. When stars spin hard enough for a few lucky people on earth to get caught up in their cosmic whirl. Sometimes wind just feels like weather. But sometimes it feels special, like it's carrying something with it. I heard voices tangled in that wind.

"Oh, sweet Daisy, don't go fearing,
When we dance along the ridge,

All the ghosts around are friendly . . .
. . . Unless you try to dig."

It's possible we were only hearing voices from the Telling Vines. But maybe, as my mom always said, we were standing in a thin place. And so, for that one magical moment, in a Gypsy Rose summer, we heard the ones we'd loved, and lost—singing. Having a front porch jamboree in heaven.

Rose petals rained madly all around us. We all stretched out our hands. We all spun in circles. I heard birdsong, wild laughter, and gasps of pure delight.

"In the buggy, Darlin' Daisy,
Now ride faster!
None can follow!
Look back once over your shoulderrrrr . . .
Wave good-bye to Blackbird Hollow!"

By the time the stormy skies had passed, the song was gone. And we were left standing among the graves, among the falling roses and glittering flowers. We were left to wonder. And to remember. Life was everywhere, all around us.

Just when you think you don't have it in you to bloom anymore, you do.

CHAPTER TWENTY-ONE

One Month after We Found the Conductor's Untold Riches

At 5:04 a.m. on the day of my twelfth birthday, Topher and Granny Blue ran into my bedroom, clanging wooden spoons against silver pots and singing "Happy Birthday."

My family is not exactly docile when it comes to special observances.

"This is the precise moment you were born, Emma Pearl!" Blue crowed. "Five-oh-four a.m.! I looked at the clock so I'd remember it forever."

Those two seemed especially giggly and antsy as they led me downstairs. I assumed they had birthday pancakes waiting for me, but I was wrong.

Set up in the dining room was my very own drum set with a swirly *E* on the bass. A scribbled note had been left for me on the snare:

Now, I'm not embarrassed to admit that the gift made me cry. Goodness knows, I've cried bucketfuls of sad tears in my lifetime. And I'm sure I'll cry many more. Happy tears were such a nice change. And it's not just the drum kit that made me happy. My heart was full at the thought of my family plotting such a perfect present for me.

I ran at Topher and Blue with my arms open wide, hugging them tightly. "I'll find every dancing song hidden in those drums," I promised.

While Blue made birthday breakfast downstairs, I snuggled Bearclaw and looked at my page in the Book of Days. I hadn't filled out the page since that first frantic night's ramblings . . . because how in the world do I sum up an adventure on a page?

Beside the book was a recent issue of the *Tailfeather*, with Earl Chance, Cody Belle, and me on the front page. We were standing behind the trunk we found in the caves below the Boneyard Cafe. We'd barely caught our breath from that adventure before people started coming in droves to tour the cemetery . . . and the caves beneath the cafe. They'd stay for a fried banana sandwich and, of course, the Boneyard Brew.

"You did it, Emma," Cody Belle said to me one day, after an especially large tour group waved good-bye. "You saved the cafe."

I couldn't help but smile. I mean, I wasn't the only one who saved the cafe. I had some help from my friends. And a funny old crow. And the long-ago dearly departed. When the State of Tennessee finally agreed with me and said Warren Steele couldn't touch the cafe—or the nearby grounds—because of the historical significance of the place, I felt like a superhero.

I felt like a Wildflower.

I bounced out of the bed and pulled my blinds. Penny Lane sat fluffed and steadfast in her tree outside the window.

I pushed open the glass and grinned at my faithful bird. "Morning, Penny."

"I'll put your keys in the fridge," she squawked back.

I laughed. Penny Lane looked down her long beak at me. She blinked her beady eyes and crooked her head, as if she wanted to know why in the world I still hadn't written something in the book.

"Because the Big Empty is still here," I whispered, tapping my fingertip over my heart. "I thought it would go away once I fulfilled my destiny. But it's still here."

Birthdays are the worst when you've lost someone you love. Other days are that way, too, of course. Tuesdays. Fridays. Sunday afternoons. Holidays and school picture day and rainy days. There's at least a few lonely minutes hiding in every day, once you've said good-bye to someone you love. But birthdays are fierce.

I closed my eyes and imagined my mom was there, lighting the candles on a giant pile of pancakes downstairs.

I imagined her kissing me on the cheek and declaring the truth of the situation. "Someone loves you, Emma Pearl. Someone will always love you."

Then I realized that I wasn't imagining her voice at all.

I heard her.

I opened my eyes to find a Telling Vine, blooming up the trellis outside my window. A warm tear rolled down my face as I pulled the bell-shaped flower toward me. I held it to my ear. And listened to my mama's voice:

"I'm connected to you by words on a page,
Connected to you by warm, summer days,
Connected to you by secrets we keep,
Connected to you in dreams when you sleep."

"That's our song," I said to Penny Lane, as if she'd actually answer me. "That's my mama. She left me a song." I wiped the tears off my face with my sleeve. And I pulled the flower to my ear again.

"I'm connected to you with each breath you take,
I'm connected to you in new memories you make,
And someday, far away, when the last story ends,
I'll be there, sweet Emma, and we'll dance again.

Someone loves you, Emma Pearl. Someone will always love you."

Bear whimpered at my ankle. I let go of the vine and picked up my pup, snuggling her close to me. I could still hear my mom's song faintly, repeating as if it really didn't end.

And a thought occurred to me, a hopeful thought.

Maybe the Telling Vines are exactly as Uncle Peri said. Maybe they carry messages. Maybe they're nature's own email system.

Or maybe, as Cody Belle would say, they're a sacred echo. I know some people think of angels and harps and rich stuff when they think of heaven. But I thought about my mom—barefoot on a back porch, her hair blowing long around her face. She's strumming a guitar that never goes out of tune. She's singing a song that doesn't end. She's thinking of me. I'm thinking of her.

Maybe we never really lose the ones we love.

Maybe we're connected, always.

Granny Blue declared that night's jamboree a Birthday Spectacular. Because the weather was warm, and because the cafe was packed, we let crowds flow out into the front yard and the graveyard, too.

When the crowd had finally gone home—mostly—I sat

on the back porch steps with the Book of Days in my lap. I heard the screen door shut behind me as Waverly and Topher stepped out on the porch.

"Hey, Emma," Waverly said as she came down the stairs. "I was just telling your brother that I saw people dancing out here earlier. Dancing in a graveyard. That's bizarre. Not as bizarre as having a graveyard for a backyard . . . but still."

Topher laughed, and tousled my hair as he bounded down the steps. "It's not that bizarre." Topher swung his arm around Waverly's waist. When he spun her in a circle, I noticed she'd tucked a red rose into her hair.

Cody Belle flopped down on one side of me, and looped her arm through mine. "Greetings, BFF."

Earl Chance settled in on my other side. Even though Earl talked now, he was still a boy of few words. He pointed to the book. "Want us to, uh, leave you alone? For just a minute?"

"You can stay," I said. "It's just that I have no clue what to write in here." I'd erased all my penciled scribbles, but all I had so far was just:

Emma Pearl Casey

But what would I write? What would my story be?

The Drummer?

The Expert Tour Guide?

The Treasure Seeker?

Those were all things I did. But it's hard to find a word that summarizes your destiny.

And it didn't seem right, taking any kind of credit for a heroic deed that wasn't all mine.

"Maybe I shouldn't write anything," I said. "Maybe that's my contribution to the Book of Days—'Dear future daughters in my wacky family: You are peachy just the way you are.'"

"What'd Blue write?" Cody Belle asked.

"She wrote about boxing gloves," I said. "Then she ripped her page out because she didn't think she'd fulfilled her destiny. And my mom wrote about her guitar."

So I flipped to my mom's page but stopped before I got there. Blue did have an entry in the Book of Days. It had been taped in, with duct tape, no less. The handwriting was unmistakably messy and Blue-like:

Bluebell Althea

Grandmother to Topher and Emma Pearl

I, Granny Blue, had the dream of my ancestors in the year of 1962.
By some standards,
I have done at least a few extraordinary things.
At least, that's what I thought.

But then I held Topher Maine.
And then I held Emma Pearl.
I watched them grow up.
I saw them bloom.
That extraordinary duo
is responsible for giving me the greatest days of my life.
So to future generations I say:
Every day you live is a day for dreaming.
Every day is a day for adventuring.
And every day is for sharing with people you love,
because love's all that lasts.
It's the only thing we carry out of this world.
It connects us all, in the end.

I wiped away the tear before it trembled down my face. "She said we're her extraordinary destiny—Topher and me."

Cody Belle elbowed me. "I always knew Granny Blue was really a softie."

"I know what you should write," Earl said.

"Then write it for me," I said, handing him the book.

He wrote:

Emma Pearl Casey
Friend to Earl Chance

And then my best friend leaned over and added:

And to Cody Belle Chitwood

"That's perfect," I said. "That's exactly what I want my legacy to be:

Emma Pearl Casey

A True and Faithful Friend."

"I have one bit of bad news," Cody Belle sighed. "It's about the stupid zoning laws. They changed again. And . . . I'll be at school with you and Earl." She grinned. "Forget Beretta and her minions. We'll be together. We'll have a Daisy Brigade!"

"Stop." Earl held up his hand. "We can't call it Daisy Brigade."

"Better idea," I said. "We have our own Club Pancake."

Cody Belle squealed and hugged me tight. Earl laughed and rolled his eyes.

I don't like to be morbid, but when you work in a graveyard and you come from a family of prodigies, it's hard not to think about what you'll be remembered for.

So this is what I've decided:

In the eyes of many people, I may never live an extraordinary life.

But I will love in extraordinary ways. And I hope I choose to always see the best in people.

She believed in magical things: buried treasure, skeleton keys, and Telling Vines. She loved.

I took a deep breath and added these words to the Book of Days:

*In my twelfth year, I had the great dream of my
ancestors.*

*I dreamed of a key
and a bundle of flowers—
a daisy, a violet, and a single red rose.
And because of that dream,
I found a song that someone left behind,
a buried treasure too wonderful for words,
and two friends I'll treasure for the rest of my life.
Best I can tell (though I might amend this someday),
I know my destiny is to bring people together.
To help lonely hearts find a place where they belong.
Believe me, future Wildflower:
You are living an extraordinary life,
day by day by glorious day.
Never doubt your starry aim.*

The sweet sound of a familiar fiddle made us all look up.

Topher was playing his violin under the tall oak, while
Waverly Valentine watched with her hands clasped over her
heart.

"I'll bet the long-ago dearly departed are grateful for a
song," I said.

Cody Belle grinned. "The dearly here-on-the-porch like
it, too."

Topher pulled the bow across the strings in long, fluid motions. The song he played reminded me of an old hymn, a bittersweet song full of sadness . . . but also hope.

Club Pancake came around the corner then, holding bundles of flowers and mugs of Boneyard Brew. Granny Blue saw me on the porch step, and winked. Uncle Peri followed Greta to the statue of the fallen soldier. Greta kissed a folded piece of paper and passed it on to Periwinkle. Peri tucked it securely into the soldier's hand. Bear pounced among the headstones, more interested in a yellow butterfly than an old grave.

Penny Lane swooped through the trees in a gentle black flutter. Crows might not have much of a singing voice, but Penny Lane's good at watching over us all. Fireflies blinked across the graves, and into the woods.

As for me, I closed the Book of Days.

And I held those stories tight against my chest.

With every turn of a page, and every beat of my heart, and every day ahead of me, I was connected to all the women who came before me.

"Listen," Cody Belle whispered softly. "I think I hear the song . . . do you hear it?"

I closed my eyes and listened. Maybe it was a song we heard that night.

Maybe it was only the wind.

ACKNOWLEDGMENTS

My heart is spinning with gratitude as I think about the people who've added their time and creativity to Emma's adventure.

First—thank *you* for taking the time to read this story. As I've visited schools, libraries, and bookstores over the past few years, I've been especially inspired by the creativity and kindness of young readers whom I've met. I hope you never doubt your starry aim.

I'm also grateful to my lovely agent, Suzie Townsend, for believing this story deserved to be book-shaped. She's passionate, thoughtful, and has a knack for sending the most perfectly timed encouragement, which means so much to me. I'm grateful for the entire team at New Leaf Literary: Joanna Volpe, Kathleen Ortiz, Pouya Shahbazian, Danielle Barthel, Jackie Lindert, Jess Dallow, Mackenzie Brady, Jaida Temperly, Chris McEwen, and Dave Caccavo. Thanks for letting me be a Leafy.

My editor, Mallory Kass, is a combination of enthusiasm, vision, and imagination that I can only describe as the best magic. Sheila Marie Everett, a publicity wizard, has coordinated many fun opportunities to share stories, and she's helped me pick up some courage along the way. I'm grateful for their kindness and their funniness. I am also grateful to many more brilliant people at Scholastic, including: Lori Benton, Tracy van Straaten, David Levithan, Bess Braswell, Whitney Steller, Rebekah Wallin, Nina Goffi, Lizette Serrano, Emily Heddleson, Antonio Gonzalez and Michelle Campbell. Thank you, Jana Haussman, and the entire team at Book Fairs, for keeping my stories on your sparkly silver shelves. And I am a major fangirl of the passionate, generous, and wonderful folks who make up the Scholastic sales team. Working with all of you is a dream.

I'm grateful for booksellers, who spend their days matching the right book with the right reader, to librarians and teachers who've given my characters a home in their classrooms, and to my #NerdyBookClub friends for pulling me into a community where geeking out over books is acceptable and expected. I'm also grateful for teachers and mentors who've been part of my life, and encouraged me to keep writing.

Like Emma, I believe home is more about friends and family than a physical location. I'm forever grateful that I got to spend many years with grandparents who were vivid storytellers. Words can't express how thankful I am for my own Club Pancake: Mom, Dad, Bridgett, Chase, Ed, Erin, and Andy. I'm also indebted to my Cody Belles—Melanie, Hannah, Kristin, and Sarah—for always making me feel brave. My friend Jeff Zentner, a brilliant storyteller, was kind enough to read an early draft of this novel and offer feedback. I can't wait for his books to be out in the world. And many thanks and treats are due to my fuzzy BFF, Biscuit, who makes sure my days are full of sweet snuggles, long walks, and squeaky toys.

And above all, I'm grateful to God—for love that never turns me loose, and for hope that finds me even on the darkest days.

I wish I could go on a treasure hunt with every person listed here, and give them big mugs of Boneyard Brew. And I wish I could tuck these words into a Telling Vine and hide it for them to find in the pages of this book:

You are a wonder and you are wonderful. I am so grateful for you.

ABOUT THE AUTHOR

Natalie Lloyd lives in Chattanooga, Tennessee. She collects old books, listens to bluegrass music, and loves exploring quirky mountain towns with her dog, Biscuit. Her first book, *A Snicker of Magic*, was an ALA Notable Children's Book, a *New York Times Book Review* Editors' Choice, and a *Parents* magazine Best Children's Book. You can visit her online at www.natalielloyd.com and follow her on Twitter at @_natalielloyd.

ABOUT THE AUTHOR

ence McCauley is an award-winning writer living in
k City. In 2014, he won the New Pulp Award for Best
nd Best Short Story for *A Bullet's All it Takes*. His
ries have been featured in *Thuglit, Shotgun Honey,*
Noir, and *Matt Hilton's Action: Pulse Pounding Tales*
2. He recently compiled *Grand Central Noir,* an
y where all proceeds go directly to God's Love We
 nonprofit organization in New York City. He has
wo acclaimed historical crime thrillers, *Prohibition*
Burn, both of which are available from Polis Books.

d him online at www.terrencepmccauley.com
and @tmccauley_nyc.

---

on them whenever you need it." The Dean tried a smile. "I'd
wish you luck, but you make your own, so I'll save my breath.
Just know you have my complete support and I look forward
to seeing results."

"And soon," Jason added. "Very soon."

Neither of them offered to shake hands, so neither did
Hicks. He and Roger simply stood up and walked out of the
kitchen.

Jason always had been a last word freak.

ROGER TOOK A cab back to his club and offered to open
a bottle of champagne to celebrate. He even offered to
put the men in leather hoods in another room. But Hicks
declined. He wanted to walk for a bit, anyway.

He'd heard everything the Dean had told him. He knew
the support he'd thrown behind him. In all his years in the
University, he'd never seen him do that for anyone.

He should've been happy or at least excited about all of
this, but he wasn't. He didn't feel a thing and knew he never
would. He rarely felt anything, which was what had made
him ideal for the kind of work he did. The work was all he
had. He'd never wanted anything else.

He pulled out his handheld and called someone he figured
would understand. She picked up just before the phone went
to voicemail.

"Why are you calling?" she asked. "What's wrong?"

"Who said anything's wrong? I know we didn't set the
world on fire the other night, but I still wanted to call and
thank you. This was the first chance I had to do it."

"A gentleman," she said. He heard the smile in her voice. "How chivalrous of you. How are you doing?"

"Busy week," he said. "Lot happened, but it turned out okay in the end, I guess. I was wondering if you were still in New York. Maybe we could meet for a drink, seeing as how well our last drink turned out."

"Now you're just being silly," she said. "You know I'm still in town. You know everything, remember?"

"No, I didn't know, but I'm glad you are. And you're wrong about me knowing everything. I don't know if you're going to say yes."

"I think you did. How does the Bull and Bear sound? Five o'clock?"

"Let's say the King Cole Bar at the St. Regis," Hicks said. "You know I don't like going to the same bar twice in a row."

"Of course. Proprieties must be observed. See you there at five."

She hung up the phone and Hicks put the handheld back in his pocket. Enough work for one day.

A light snow began to fall and some of it had already begun to stick on the cars and sidewalk. Another storm was rolling in.

He used to like the snow, but didn't anymore.

THE END

ACKNOWLEDGI

Thanks to Maura Lynch, Tessa
Debora Oliveira, Melissa Gardella and
invaluable insight on this book in its

Thanks to my resident gun exp
Viljoen for their advice on the variou
book, especially Blackie who first t
Alaskan. They had me at 'it can core

Thanks to Lorin and Micheal
Lomax, Eric Frank, Kathy English, C
Christine Voss Copp USAF, C.J. Carp
Donohue, Wesley Gibson, Liz Thale
Charles Salzberg, Will D., Phyllis S
King, Mike Reyes, Mae Patel, Rich
Mark Mannix, Donna Evans, Tani
their constant encouragement and

Thanks to Mike, Pat, Juan, th
Adams, Mark and all the gang at t
New York City for all the great tim

Thanks to Todd Robinson,
Davis, Paul Bishop, Jack Getze an
me when a lot of people told me
found me at a low-ebb in my writi
going.

Thank you to James Grady
Condor' and the movie based
Condor' caused me to fall in lov
and inspired me to try my hand

Thank you to Owen Laukk
Tim O'Mara for their generous s

Thanks to my agent and p
the Doug Grad Literary Agency
Irishman on course. Thanks to
was gracious enough to allow
growing Polis family.

And thank you to Arcenia
this would be possible.

My love and gratitude to y